I Never

I
Never

LAURA
HOPPER

Houghton Mifflin Harcourt
Boston · New York

hmhbooks.com

Book design by Chrissy Kurpeski
The text was set in Bembo Std.

The Library of Congress has cataloged the hardcover edition as follows:
Names: Hopper, Laura, author.
Title: I never / Laura Hopper.
Description: Boston ; New York : Houghton Mifflin Harcourt, 2017. | Summary: After learning that her seemingly happy parents are separating, and that a popular senior is interested in her, seventeen-year-old Janey King's priorities shift from track, school, friends, and family to something more.
Identifiers: LCCN 2016058441 (print) | LCCN 2017028555 (ebook)
Subjects: | CYAC: Coming of age—Fiction. | Best friends—Fiction. | Friendship—Fiction. | Dating (Social customs)—Fiction. | Sex—Fiction. | High schools—Fiction. | Schools—Fiction. | Family problems—Fiction.
Classification: LCC PZ7.1.H663 (ebook) | LCC PZ7.1.H663 Iaan 2017 (print) | DDC [Fic]—dc23
LC record available at https://lccn.loc.gov/2016058441

ISBN: 978-1-328-66378-8 hardcover
ISBN: 978-1-328-59587-4 paperback

Printed in the United States of America
DOC 10 9 8 7 6 5 4 3 2 1
4500755776

FOR NATE, SAMANTHA, AND HENRY,
WHO INSPIRE ME.

FOR MY MOM AND DAD, WHO BELIEVE IN ME.

CHAPTER ONE

HAPPY FREAKIN' NEW YEAR. Did they really think this was a good time to do this? Really? Here we are in beautiful Cabo San Lucas, where I'm enjoying a much-needed break from the stress that junior year of high school brings. At our supposedly celebratory New Year's Eve dinner, they drop the bomb. "Separating." "Splitting up." We all know those are euphemisms for the dreaded *D* word. They promise it's amicable, whatever that means. They say they've drifted apart and don't want to grow old without that spark.

I'm speechless, but maybe not shocked. I guess I thought they were happy in a best-friends kind of way. Not sure I gave it much thought, really. They get along fine, but it's not like they stare lovingly at each other across the dinner table, or sneak little kisses as they pass each other in the hallway. But, are there actually couples in their forties who have been married for more than twenty years who are crazy in love? Do they really expect rainbows and butterflies this late in the game? Isn't that for teenagers? Not that I've had the whole magical experience myself. I'm seventeen and still haven't delved into that part of my life.

Yes, I know plenty of seventeen-year-olds are dating, are having sex, are maybe even in love. It really hasn't occurred to me that I might be missing out on something. I don't think of myself as a late bloomer; I just haven't felt ready for all that. Maybe it's because there's no one I've met who seems worth the trouble: missing time with friends, figuring out how to add a boyfriend to an already very busy schedule. He'd have to be exceptional, and I haven't met anyone exceptional at La Jolla High. Yet.

I just think sex should mean something. After all, it's my body, the one body I have, which has to last forever. Why would I let someone have that kind of access without being pretty important in the scheme of things? I don't want to let someone get that close to me only to have that person ultimately mean nothing in my life. I think too much.

I walk with my mom and dad from the hotel restaurant through the lobby. My parents each hold one of my hands like I'm tiny and they're going to say "one, two, three, wheeee" and whisk me high into the air.

The lobby of the hotel is decorated with twinkly holiday lights and streamers. Noisemakers overflow from buckets strategically placed on tables and credenzas. Other hotel guests are dressed festively for the occasion. Some guys are in suits and ties, others in Hawaiian shirts. Many women wear short, sexy dresses, probably purchased for the sole purpose of ringing in the New Year. I feel slightly underdressed in my blue jeans and flip-flops. The sound of champagne corks popping resonates through the air at regular intervals.

In the dimly lit piano bar, an old guy with dyed black hair and sunglasses sits at a baby grand piano. Next to him, a woman stands at the microphone in a super-tight red dress that clashes with her orange lipstick. They perform classic songs that are probably too old-fashioned even for my parents. My dad snags a tall table with three stools, and within seconds, a waiter with a cardboard top hat arrives and asks what we'd like to drink. My parents order champagne and I ask for a Sprite. I know my mom will give me a sip of her champagne and it will tickle my nose and taste bitter, but at least I'll have the all-important New Year's Eve beverage.

Their words are still ricocheting in my head. Divorce. I'm a statistic. Last year, on the debate team, we argued the topic *Should divorce be made even easier to obtain, or are there social and moral reasons to discourage it?* I was assigned the opposition side, which means I had to take the position that people should have to work harder at their marriages before getting divorced. I remember standing at the podium, shoulders back, chin up, stating confidently, "It is far less damaging for children to live in an imperfect, yet stable and secure, household than to suffer the disintegration of the only family they know." That's me now, insecure and unstable. Incidentally, my team won that round of the debate.

When the orange lips start singing "Fly Me to the Moon," my dad takes my mom's hand and pulls her up to dance. They hold each other close, smiling and whispering in each other's ears. And yet, they're getting divorced. I'm so confused.

CHAPTER TWO

GAIN, I FEEL like a little girl, wedged between my mom and dad in our coach seats in row twenty-one on Aeromexico. My dad's a pilot, and he gets really good deals on airline tickets. I'm still waiting for the day we get to fly first class. I've got my phone in my lap and Coldplay blasting through my earbuds, making it impossible for me to engage in conversation. We haven't even left the gate, but I think it's important to establish the tone of the journey home so that my parents don't get any ideas about a two-hour heart-to-heart reminding me that we're still a family and they love me so very much, blah blah blah.

I am glad to be heading home and getting back into the routine of school, friends, debate, and track team. I begin to wonder, slightly fearfully, how things are going to change. I'm not so big on change. I tend to stick with friends and hobbies. I don't take big fashion risks. I've had the same all-one-length hair to the middle of my back since I was ten. I realize, sitting on the runway, that I haven't yet made a New Year's resolution. Maybe I should have a better attitude about change. I resolve to embrace new things, take more chances. Then I muse about whether anyone sticks to their New Year's resolutions. Probably not.

Other passengers are making their way down the aisle, carrying absurdly huge suitcases that they're going to try to cram into the overhead bins. People are sporting sunburns and wearing silver jewelry they probably bought from salesmen on the beach after extensive bartering. Everyone looks relaxed following their peaceful vacations, yet stressed about the hassle of a day of travel.

The flight attendant announces over the loudspeaker that we all must find our seats so we can push back from the gate. I look up to see which selfish travelers are still having trouble getting themselves settled and I look right into the eyes of Luke Hallstrom. Not just Luke Hallstrom, but Luke Hallstrom with a golden tan.

Luke is a senior at La Jolla High School. I know him because he's also on the track team. I'd probably know him anyway because he's tall and handsome and athletic and it's virtually impossible not to know Luke Hallstrom. Luke is always surrounded by other athletic, popular guys and at least one beautiful girl. It seems that whenever he's walking around school, he always has his big strong arm draped over a girl who looks incredibly happy to be wrapped in that arm. Most girls at my school would feel lucky to take that walk down the school hallway, tucked in close to Luke. As much as I can appreciate his hand-some face and impeccable hair, I have never had a crush on Luke. The only crush I've ever really had was when I was a freshman and Tyler Stone lent me his umbrella.

Tyler was a junior at the time, and he was the editor of the school paper. I read his articles religiously, thinking he was wise and witty and clearly destined for greatness. One afternoon, I was waiting in the rain for my mom to pick me up, and Tyler was driving out of the student parking lot. He stopped in front of me, leaned out the window, and handed me his black compact umbrella. No words were exchanged. I was immediately smitten. I re-member plotting and planning with my friends about the ideal time and place to return it, and the exact words to say when I handed it to him. Days later, as I approached him at his locker, reminding myself of the clever speech I had rehearsed many times, all I managed to say was "Uh, thanks" while I handed over the umbrella I had taken such good care of. He looked at me like he had no rec-ollection of our previous interaction, the same one I had played over and over in my head. The umbrella seemed to jog his memory enough for him to say, "Oh, yeah, you bet." That was it. My crush lasted the rest of the year. We never spoke again.

Now here I am staring right at Luke Hallstrom. He's staring back. I can practically see the gears turning in his head. He's sure that I look familiar, but he can't quite place how he knows me. Were we staying at the same hotel in

Mexico? Do I go to his school? Did we hook up? He has probably hooked up with so many girls that he can easily forget who's on that list. Then he seems to remember how we know each other, and he smiles. His tan makes his teeth look really white. I smile back. He takes his seat in the row directly in front of me and all I see of him is the top of his head with its curly brown hair. Chris Martin sings in my ears *"Life goes on, it gets so heavy."*

An hour into the flight, I remain in my seat, eyes closed, blocking out the rest of the world by focusing on the music emanating from my phone. "Wherever I Go," one of my favorite songs by OneRepublic, comes on. I turn up the volume ever so slightly, drowning out the hum of the airplane.

"No easy love could ever make me feel the same. Make me feel the same." Something—I don't know what; perhaps a sense that I am being stared at—makes me open my eyes. Sure enough, Luke Hallstrom has turned around in his seat and is looking right at me. He smiles in a way that makes me paranoid. Do I have something on my face? And then it dawns on me. I take the earbud out of my left ear and turn to my mom.

"Was I singing out loud?" I ask.

"Yes, you were," she answers.

"Why didn't you stop me?" I ask, totally annoyed that she would let me embarrass myself that way.

"You weren't bothering anyone," she says, as though

my singing out loud is quite possibly the cutest thing she's ever heard.

There is no way I'm going to school on Monday. Luke Hallstrom just heard me singing. And not just singing, but singing about obsession. Between that and the divorce, this has been the worst trip in the history of family vacations.

As soon as we land at the airport in San Diego, and my phone finally has a signal, I text Brett.

I'll be home in forty-five minutes. Meet me there. I have news.

Thank goodness for reliable, dependable Brett, who texts back within seconds.

Good or bad? Vanilla or chocolate?

Bad. Chocolate.

Even though my house in San Diego is only about a thousand miles from our hotel in Cabo, it feels like I've traveled a far greater distance since New Year's Eve, which was only two days ago. It's so nice to be in the back seat of the taxi, seeing the familiar neighborhood streets, the shopping malls, the minivans. The cab pulls up in front of our house and I am relieved to see Brett leaning against his RAV4, holding two frozen chocolate concoctions, complete with whipped cream and purple straws. Ahh, it's good to be back in the USA.

Brett and I have been friends since the second grade.

We've been doing homework together since we were learning our math facts. He's the only friend I have who went to the same elementary school, middle school, and now high school. We know each other's parents, each other's social media passwords, and, clearly, each other's favorite coffee drinks.

Some people at school don't understand my friendship with Brett. They assume we *like* like each other because we hang out so much. Neither Brett nor I has ever been in a real relationship. Even though Brett also says he doesn't care about having a girlfriend, I can tell he's lying. Our friend Danielle has a boyfriend, and they're always making out at school or holding hands at the lunch tables, and, every once in a while, I catch Brett staring longingly at them. He's had a few dates and has hooked up with a couple of girls, which is a lot more than I've done, but he seems to envy the whole boyfriend-girlfriend thing. He'd be a good boyfriend because he's loyal and generous, and he's not super busy with sports like a lot of other eleventh-grade boys. He'd be ready, willing, and able to make out at school and hold hands at the lunch tables.

Brett and I take our beverages to the backyard and sit by the fire pit.

"Janey, what's the big news? Did you find a hot Latin lover in Cabo?" He doesn't waste much time.

"Hardly." Checking to make sure the doors are closed and we have privacy, I tell him about my parents' pending split. Brett's jaw drops. He gives me a big hug that I

didn't realize I needed until this very minute. The floodgates open and tears pour down my face. Brett lets me cry.
It takes a long time before I can get myself together. Just
as I take a huge breath, indicating that I'm back on track,
my mom pops her head out the back door.

"You kids all right? Need some snacks?"

"All good, Mrs. King, thanks." Brett handles it, knowing I may still have a rocky crying voice.

As soon as the door shuts, we share a look and burst out
laughing. Why is it that so many things a parent says are
wrong, weird, or extremely annoying? On the other hand,
even though they often bug me to death, the thought
of my parents not being together, as parents should be,
is making me so sad. I guess I'm caught somewhere between needing them desperately and needing my independence even more.

CHAPTER THREE

O N THE FIRST DAY of school after winter break, Brett drives me into the parking lot, where Sloan is waiting for me, as usual. This has been our routine all year long. The three of us—Danielle, Sloan, and I—meet in the parking lot and walk into school together. Sometimes Brett walks with us; sometimes he meets up with his buddies. He can always tell when we need him to leave us to our girl time.

Sloan and Danielle are my best friends. We're different from one another and yet so well matched. Sloan is absolutely boy crazy. She develops crushes as quickly as most teenagers develop pimples. She spends class time gawking at boys. No matter the class, she can usually find someone gawk-worthy. It takes great talent, or maybe a seasoned eye, to be able to discover something to lust after in any given situation.

Sloan has two older sisters, so she was exposed to a lot of information about guys and sex pretty early on. She was the first girl to get her period, and the first to French kiss. Sloan is beautiful and curvy, and she attracts a lot of attention wherever she goes. Boys love Sloan, and Sloan loves that boys love her. It's a mutual admiration society. It's fascinating to watch her in action.

Danielle is the mother figure in our threesome. She has thirteen-year-old twin brothers who are always getting into some kind of trouble or another. Danielle's parents are a little bit older, and I think the twins completely exhaust them. They are constantly attending meetings with the twins' teachers or coaches to discuss the boys' latest in a string of bad choices. As a result, Danielle has had to figure out how to take care of things on her own so as not to further burden her mom and dad.

Danielle has been dating Charlie since September. I don't think she even noticed Charlie freshman or sophomore year, but at the beginning of this year, Sloan (always the dependable source of valuable intel) reported that Charlie had a huge crush on Danielle. After giving it about ten minutes' thought, Danielle decided that she liked him back and—poof!—they became boyfriend and girlfriend. Now they can't keep their hands off each other, which can get a little tiresome if I'm just trying to do a last-minute cram for my trigonometry test.

As I approach Sloan, she greets me with a hug and an extended lower lip, which is her way of reminding me that she's sad about the news I shared via text when I returned from Mexico. I shrug as if to say *What are you gonna do?* She jumps right into cheer-me-up mode.

"I hear the chemistry teacher who is subbing while Ms. Stacer is on maternity leave is hot."

"On that note . . ." Brett says as he peels away and heads toward the school building. Brett tends to do a lot of eye-rolling when it comes to girls' meaningless crushes on people he deems unworthy.

"How would you even hear that?" I ask Sloan.

"He used to teach at Muirlands." Sloan has up-to-the-minute updates on random subjects. Usually gossip, usually about boys, sometimes useful, often not.

Before Sloan has a chance to delve into more details about the teacher, we see Danielle arrive in her mom's SUV. When she opens the door to jump out of the passenger seat, we can hear the twins fighting in the back seat. I get my second sympathy hug of the morning. I accept it gladly. The three of us begin the walk toward the main building and our first class. Being back in my routine is comforting.

"How are things at home?" Sloan wants to know.

"Weird. They act like everything's fine. They're still sleeping in the same room and sharing the newspaper while they eat their corn flakes. The only difference is that they're being super nice to me and constantly checking to see how I'm feeling."

"Weird," Danielle agrees.

"I just don't need the distraction right now," I add. "Track's about to start, I have a debate on Saturday, and I need to get straight As this semester to even have a shot at Stanford."

Sloan stops in her tracks, adjusts her ponytail, and licks her lips as if to make sure her gloss hasn't evaporated. Danielle and I look to see the cause of Sloan's diversion. Luke Hallstrom is walking right toward us. He's with two girls and another guy. One of the girls jumps on Luke's back for an impromptu piggyback ride. He's caught up in conversation, laughing and still flaunting his south-of-the-border glow. Just as he's about to pass us, he looks straight at me.

"What's up?" he says.

"Hey" is all I can think to say in response.

And then he's gone. Sloan is practically shaking.

"Holy crap. What was that about?" she asks in shock.

"Nothing. We were on the same plane home from Cabo," I say, attempting to calm her down.

"I can't believe you waited this long to tell me."

"Oh, sorry," I say sarcastically. "Maybe I've had other things on my mind."

"He's almost worth running around and around that track like a brain-dead hamster," Sloan says, turning around to get another glimpse of Luke.

"Oh, please, you couldn't run one mile without collapsing," I say.

Danielle chimes in, "Well, if she collapses, maybe Luke will come to her rescue and give her mouth-to-mouth."

"That, my friend, is a brilliant idea." Sloan seems to be seriously considering it.

"Well, there are optional workouts after school before the season starts," I add. "Feel free to join me, because I plan to be there every day. Anything to avoid the weirdness at home."

As we approach the wall of lockers, Charlie appears out of nowhere and practically tackles Danielle. They haven't seen each other for the full two weeks of break because Danielle was visiting her grandparents in Palm Springs. Charlie turns her around, backs her up against the lockers, and starts kissing her with unbridled desire. I try to look away, but it's like a car crash: You don't want to see the blood and guts, but you just can't pull your eyes from the wreckage. It's as though Danielle and Charlie are totally unaware of where they are and who's nearby. I can't imagine being so into someone that I would kiss with such passion in the middle of the science hallway. Sloan and I leave so they can make out in peace, or whatever peace you can find at eight o'clock on a January morning at school.

CHAPTER FOUR

AFTER SCHOOL, I go to the locker room to change into workout clothes. I shove my backpack into my locker and start to take off my jeans and Converse. The girls on the basketball and soccer teams are all there, getting ready to head to practice. So many of these girls, the seniors in particular, look like women. Their bodies, their hair, the way they dress. I feel like a little kid next to them.

Many of them have real bodies, the ultra-coveted boobs and butts that girls show off on Instagram to hundreds of *likes.* I, on the other hand, am severely lacking in that department. And since I'm already seventeen, I don't think I can hope to ever be blessed with those assets. Where these girls have cleavage that spills out of their demi-cup bras and full round butts that sit up high under their thongs, I have A-cup boobs and not much of a behind at all.

As the other girls change out of their jeans, skirts, and leggings and into their shorts and jog tops, I notice their delicate and colorful lace bras and thong underwear.

Clearly, these girls are doing their very best to be sexy. I wonder if they're selecting underwear for themselves or to impress someone else. I've never considered purchasing a bra for its aesthetic value. If it's comfortable and doesn't show through my T-shirt, it's just right for me. I suppose it has something to do with the fact that I've never undressed in front of someone I was hoping to dazzle.

As I sit on the concrete floor lacing up my Nike Air Max shoes, I continue to observe the senior girls as though I'm conducting a study. They rub sunscreen onto their long legs and toned arms and pull their shiny hair into smooth ponytails before they do a thorough check in the mirror and saunter out. I take a moment to inspect my own reflection, which I rarely take the time to do. Frankly, I'm not that impressed.

My running shorts have seen better days; they sort of hang on my hips, and the drawstring is frayed. My hair is twisted haphazardly on top of my head, showing no evidence whatsoever of use of a brush or other grooming utensil. My body, a typical runner's body, with its muscular legs and narrow shoulders, seems supremely unsexy to me. Before letting myself get too discouraged, I look away and head to the track. After all, who's even looking?

I walk down the steps, past the bleachers.

"Pssst. Janey."

I glance up. Sloan sits in the first row, drinking a vitaminwater. She leans over the railing.

"What are you doing?" I ask.

"Checking out the scenery. Best show in town."

I turn to see what she's watching. Luke Hallstrom stretches near the long jump pit. I roll my eyes at Sloan. Some things never change.

"Why don't you join us?" I suggest.

"I don't look good in sweat," she answers with a flip of her hair.

"See ya." I can't help but be amused by her one-track mind and, in this case, her good taste. Sloan is the girl who some parents would refer to as *fast*. They'd probably be shocked to learn that she's technically a virgin. She loves to go to parties and hook up with guys. In fact, her mantra is *everything but*. She frequently talks about all the times she's done *everything but*.

Danielle and I started calling Sloan *E.B.* because of all her stories about doing *everything but,* and the nickname just stuck. Sometimes people hear us call her *E.B.* and ask about the origin of the nickname. We never share.

As sexy and fast as Sloan appears to be, she does not want to have sex until she's in an exclusive relationship. Sadly, her virgin status is less widely known than her reputation for having a lot of fun with guys.

I join the kids on the track team who are stretching on the field. Coach Chow offers these workouts so those of us who don't have other winter sports can get in shape for the season.

"Let's start with an eight hundred warm-up," Chow says as I approach.

As much as I like my teammates, I'd rather run alone. I hit the track and get started at a fairly fast pace. As I round the first turn, I hear footsteps approaching and can feel a body closing in on my right. I'm not used to being passed, so I quickly turn to see who it is. Luke Hallstrom. If I'm going to get passed, it might as well be by him. The funny thing is, he's not passing me. He's just running right alongside me in the next lane. It's a little awkward, truth be told. He probably doesn't even see me. I'm not sure if I should drop back and let him run ahead or speed up to create some distance. Anything to avoid this weird situation where we're running side by side, saying nothing to each other.

I can't help but notice that he smells really good. Not cologne so much as a clean, soapy boy smell, which is pretty impressive this late in the day. I'm still wrestling with whether I should try to make some space between us, but it's not so easy to make a move away from Luke. He's like a magnet, making it nearly impossible for me to separate from him.

"Whoa, Janey King, you're quick," he says.

What the heck? First, he knows my name. And not just my first name, but my full name. Second, he's talking to me. Third, and I can't be certain, but I think he just complimented me. What do I say? *Thank you* seems like a lame response. *You, too,* would be flirty, and I don't really do flirty.

"Just trying to get it over with." Deflecting the praise is probably a good strategy.

"Very funny. Seriously, you're really strong and fast. I have to push myself to keep up."

"Thanks." At this point, gratitude is unavoidable. "But I could never clear a seven-foot high jump, which you can probably do in your sleep." Did I just flirt? Those words felt weird coming out of my mouth. But what choice did I have? I couldn't just keep basking in his admiration.

"Actually, I pole vault in my sleep. But that damn pole keeps waking me up."

"Ha, ha."

"So, you like OneRepublic, huh?" There it is. The most humiliating moment of my life is back to haunt me. I feel my face turn hot and red.

"I'm so embarrassed," I admit.

"Why?" he asks. "I love that song."

"Yes, but you weren't singing it out loud to a plane full of strangers."

"Hey, it was the best part of the flight," he jokes.

Is this really happening? Is Luke Hallstrom working to make conversation with me? *Why?* I wonder. I must change the subject. Anything to take the focus off my blunder. We keep running at a pretty good pace while we talk. For me, the conversation takes a lot more effort than the run.

"Where'd you stay in Mexico?" I ask.

"We rented a house. My brother and sister were on break from college. So we did the whole family thing."

"That sounds really nice."

"Yeah, but my legs didn't get as tan as yours." Holy crap. He noticed my legs. This is foreign territory for me. It sure does make the warm-up run go by quickly. Where is this coming from? Last year, we were both out here every afternoon, and he never even looked in my direction, much less at my legs. And it's not like one of those movies where one morning, I threw out my glasses, grew gigantic boobs, and returned to school walking in slow motion down the hallway with bouncy hair to match my bouncy chest. I'm the same Janey I was sophomore year.

"I'll race you to the finish," he says and takes off. It's by far the best challenge I've ever faced. I use all the gas that's left in my tank to sprint the last quarter lap of the run. I pass him, but he stays right on my tail. I can feel him behind me. I push harder. He's still there. I finish with him right behind me. He collapses dramatically and hilariously. I stand over him.

"You okay?"

"Help me up." He extends a hand and I notice that he wears a thin brown leather braid around his wrist. I grab his hand and am surprised that it feels so soft and yet so strong. He doesn't let go so quickly. It's probably just two seconds, but it feels like an eternity. We walk over to where Chow is assembling the hurdles. Luke puts one of his heels up on a hurdle to do a hamstring stretch. I pretend to help Chow, but I surreptitiously keep an eye on Luke. I can't help but notice that his legs did get pretty tan. And he has just the right amount of hair on his legs —not too dark, not too fuzzy, just enough to seem like a man, but not a scary, hairy man. His gray La Jolla Track shirt is damp with sweat, and for some reason it's not gross. As a matter of fact, it's kinda hot. What am I thinking? Has Sloan, aka E.B., rubbed off on me in all the wrong ways?

Luke and I spend the rest of practice in our separate areas, but I feel that magnetic pull again, like something is drawing me to the long jump pit. I manage to stay in my designated spot, not an easy task.

CHAPTER FIVE

THAT NIGHT'S FAMILY DINNER is so normal, it's weird. When my dad isn't flying, we make a point to sit down and eat together. My mom teaches kindergarten, and she always said that one of the many reasons she loves her job is that it allows her to have the same hours I have and that she can be home to make dinner. Tonight, Mom made my favorite meal, chicken and biscuits, and dad announces he picked up a pint of Ben & Jerry's Phish Food. Now that I think about it, maybe this dinner is better than normal. Mom and Dad ask fewer annoying questions than usual about my day, my friends, my teachers, my track workout. They've done none of their regular pushing or pressuring about homework, tests, and debate topics.

In the two days since we've been home, there has been no talk of the demise of their marriage, no mention of someone (my dad, I presume) moving out, no one sleeping on the sofa. Maybe they were in a margarita-induced haze when they gave me the news on New Year's Eve.

Maybe they changed their minds and realized that they can't live without each other. I've always been able to speak freely with my parents, so I take it upon myself to say something.

"Is this the way it's supposed to be?"

"What do you mean?" Mom's eyes are wide with curiosity. Her eyebrows climb up her forehead.

"I mean that you guys are separating. But we're all together. And you're both being super nice. All. The. Time."

They exchange a glance. Mom nods at Dad, encouraging him to speak up.

"We want to make sure you're fine and that we don't make any sudden changes." He speaks as though I'm a time bomb that could explode at any given moment.

Mom picks up where he leaves off. "It's a stressful year for you, and we want to be helpful, not hurtful."

"Guys, I get it. I can handle it. I'll be fine."

Mom's eyes brim with prideful tears, as if I've just won the Nobel Peace Prize. "We know, and we're going to make sure we do what's best for you."

I wish I could say, *Then you wouldn't be getting divorced.* But that might interrupt the whole lovey-dovey, mushy King family moment.

I decide that the sooner I finish my Phish Food, the sooner I can get back to my room and enjoy the pleasure of my own company. And my Spanish homework. I power through the dessert, get a scorching ice cream headache, and put my bowl in the dishwasher.

"Thanks for the yummy dinner. Love you."

"Love you back," they say almost in unison.

In the comfort of my own room, I settle onto my bed. I lean back against the pile of pillows with my Spanish textbook and my laptop splayed out in front of me. I have to create a travel brochure for a Spanish-speaking country. Mexico seems too obvious. Belize, maybe. I start to research Belize, but my phone makes a *pong* noise, telling me I have new text message. I grab my phone.

Hey.

It's from a phone number I don't recognize.

Who's this? I type.

Luke shows up on my screen. Really? Is someone messing with me? There is no way that Luke Hallstrom is texting me.

Luke who?

Luke Hallstrom.

I'm not sure whether to believe this is real; how the heck did Luke get my phone number? Then I remember that the track team roster from last year has everyone's info to encourage us to carpool to meets if we don't want to ride the team bus. I pull up the roster on my computer and, sure enough, the phone numbers match.

He was on my mind this afternoon, and even this evening. I wondered if other people on the team saw us running together, and what they thought about that. They probably figured it was some kind of mistake. I wasn't really sure what I, myself, thought about that. But I know that my heart is beating really fast right now, and I'm sitting in my room all by myself with a big stupid smile spreading across my face.

Hey, I text back. *What's up?*

Just procrastinating. Don't wanna read Crime and Punishment 2 nite.

Ugh. I don't blame u. The crazy-fast heartbeat and the big stupid smile show no signs of stopping.

What r u doing? he types.

Spanish hw. Fun fun fun.

Although the last thing I'm thinking about at the moment is my Spanish homework, and while the *fun fun fun* was meant sarcastically, I am truthfully having a lot of fun right this very second.

R u going to track workout tomorrow? he asks.

I think so. R u?

Yeah. Wanna go get a juice or coffee after?

I have to take a breath before I answer with an enthusiastic *YES.* I want to make sure my response seems more casual than I feel.

Sounds good, I write.

Cool. C U tomorrow.

Can this be real? Do I really have a date with Luke? Why would he want to go out with me? I am so normal I'm practically invisible, and he is widely known and adored. Is a beverage in the afternoon even considered a real date? My first instinct is to text Sloan. I feel much too excited to keep this to myself, and I want her professional opinion on every word that was exchanged. I start to type, but then I hit the cancel button. There's a chance Sloan won't be happy for me. She has had a crush on Luke for a while. She does, however, crush on several boys at a time. But what if she gets mad or jealous? I don't want her to dampen my excitement. I decide to keep this to myself, which is not easy to do. It's also not easy to focus on homework. Or anything besides Luke.

CHAPTER SIX

I WAKE UP BEFORE my alarm goes off, which never happens. Most mornings involve my pressing the snooze button two times, stumbling into the kitchen in my pajamas, inhaling some orange juice and a bowl of Rice Krispies, and waking up while listening to NPR, which is always on while my parents eat their breakfast. After my sleepy breakfast, I typically take a two-minute shower, throw on some clothes, toss shorts and a T-shirt into a bag with my running shoes, brush my teeth and my hair, and go wait outside for Brett to pick me up.

This morning is entirely different. My eyes fly open fifteen minutes before I have to get up. I lie in bed and find myself smiling that goofy smile again. Was that text exchange a dream? I reach over and grab my phone from my nightstand and reread our texts. There it is in black and white. Although there's still a chance I'm being punked.

After a long, hot shower and a little more of my vanilla-scented body wash than I typically use, I find my best jeans, the ones I always wear when I care what I look like, which isn't that often. I put on the baby-blue hoodie I got for Christmas. It's super soft and Sloan asked to borrow it when she saw it, which makes me think it's probably good enough for the occasion. Now for the workout clothes. I decide to go with all black: black Adidas shorts and a black shirt I got from the 10K I ran in October. I can honestly say I've never planned out my track practice outfit before.

I brush my hair in the mirror and decide to leave it down. Even though I spend a few more minutes on it than I do most mornings, I realize it probably doesn't look any different than it did yesterday, which might be a good thing. My phone makes that *pong* sound again. It's Brett, and he's waiting outside. Holy crap, how is it 7:45 already? I thought I had so much extra time. I run into the kitchen and grab a cereal bar.

"Janey, do you have a second?" Dad calls from the kitchen table.

"Sorry, Daddy, Brett is waiting outside."

"You look pretty." My mom notices the difference. I really don't want to appear as though I've made extra effort. Hopefully my mom is more perceptive than my friends at school. My mom can look in my eyes and see that I have a fever without even touching my forehead.

"Oh, thanks," I say, hoping to sound as if I can't imagine why I look any prettier today than I would on any other Tuesday. I give her a quick kiss on the cheek and head out the door.

Brett and I arrive in the lot a few minutes late, thanks to me. Sloan and Danielle are waiting there. Brett, annoyed at my tardiness, rushes off to class.

"Why are you so dressed up?" Sloan knows me as well as my mother does.

"I'm in jeans and a sweatshirt," I say.

"You know what I mean."

"It's true," Danielle adds. "You look fancy . . . for you."

"Thanks a lot," I say.

"Really, what's the deal?" Sloan isn't giving up.

I want to tell them. I need to tell them. They are, after all, my best friends. But what if I tell them about my sort-of date and then it doesn't happen? What if he forgets? What if he was just kidding? What if he gets a better offer from a hotter, older girl?

"I'm going out with Luke after track." It feels so good to say it out loud. I can't contain my happiness.

"Luke who?" Danielle wants to know.

"Luke who do you think?" I say.

"Don't tell me you're talking about Luke Hallstrom." Sloan's smile is a mile wide. She's staring at me, awaiting official confirmation.

"I am."

She screams. I mean a horror-movie shrieking kind of scream. Everyone around us turns to see who got stabbed. The three of us start to laugh.

"Nothing to see here. Go about your business," Danielle assures the oglers.

"Tell us everything," Sloan coaxes.

"There's really not much to tell," I say, trying to sound casual.

"Oh, puh-leeze!" Sloan says. "If you're going out with him, then you spoke to him, and already that's a lot to tell. So hurry up, I have English in three minutes. Talk fast."

I do my best to tell the story while downplaying my excitement. I don't want my friends to make a big deal about it only to have the whole thing turn out to be nothing. I give them the facts without the emotion. The problem is they know me too well.

"Don't pretend like it's no big thing. You're wearing your new hoodie, your hair is all brushed and silky, and you're smiling like it's going out of style. It's okay to be fired up," Danielle assures me.

"Okay, I'm excited, but there's always a chance he's going to blow it off."

"Why would he do that? He asked you just last night. I promise you, not enough time has passed for him to change his mind," Danielle says.

"True," I say, trying to convince myself.

I'm really glad I told them. It's exciting to share, and so helpful to be talked off the ledge. We get to the hallway and have to go our separate ways. Danielle and Sloan each give me a hug. We don't usually hug goodbye when we're going to see one another at break in two hours, but the big news has clearly has changed the dynamic of the day.

I get to chemistry and do my best to focus on Mr. Bal

and his droning on about Rutherford's nuclear atom. I glance around at the boys in my class. Already I'm comparing them to Luke. Owen is sitting right in front of me, and his hair looks like he slept in a wind tunnel. Luke's hair is always the best kind of messy. Next to Owen is Garrett, who is sticking his pencil in his ear. I can't imagine Luke doing anything that disgusting. Down the row from me is Parker, who is trying to discreetly finish his breakfast. He pulls small pieces of waffle out of the pocket of his joggers and slips them into his mouth, hoping no one will notice. I wonder if there's syrup on that thing and what the inside of his pocket looks and smells like.

I practically have to shake myself out of this. Is this really me? Janey King? Spending class time scrutinizing boys and mentally criticizing them for not living up the standards set by Luke? I've got to get focused. This is exactly why I haven't been interested in a high school romance. It clouds the senses and messes with the brain. I vow to keep my brain on point. I zero in on Mr. Bal and the wonderfully captivating subject of the atomic model.

At lunch, the debate team is meeting in the music room to prep for this weekend's tournament. Everyone in the group, a mix of tenth-, eleventh-, and twelfth-graders, brings a lunch and spends the fifty minutes mock debating. Mr. Dawson, an English teacher, also oversees debate. He's very cool and really knows how to coach us. Debate is the only class I have with Brett, which makes it another reason I love these lunches. Brett is a fantastic debater. He makes strong arguments and can fight passionately on any subject.

"Today's resolution is," Mr. Dawson begins, "sex education in schools is advantageous."

Brett and I share a smirk.

Mr. Dawson continues, "Who would like to take this one?"

I raise my hand, as does almost everyone else. We are nothing if not an eager bunch.

"Janey, you take prop. Landon, you're on opp."

We have gathered research and prepared information on a number of different topics. We have arguments for both sides of every resolution. After ten minutes of sifting through outlines and jotting down notes, Landon, a bookish sophomore, and I move to the front of the classroom. I start. I may have trouble talking to a cute boy while jogging around a track, but I can debate anyone, anytime. Chin up, shoulders down, eye contact.

"There has been an ongoing debate ever since sex education was introduced in schools, about whether it is beneficial for young students to have such a wide range of knowledge. Sex education in schools is absolutely advantageous. Of all westernized countries, the United States has the highest percentage of teen pregnancy. If sex education is introduced in schools, students will be educated about forms of contraception, and they will be made aware of the importance of abstinence."

I look around the room, working to make eye contact

with everyone sitting there. I lock eyes with Brett, who I know is my biggest supporter.

"Another benefit of teaching sex education in schools is the reduction of sexually transmitted diseases, including HIV, among young people." I go on, discussing the appropriate ages for children to learn about sex, and note that the data suggests that many parents are not emotionally or psychologically equipped to have the necessary conversation with their kids. I get a nice round of snaps from my peers before Landon begins his argument.

"There are many disadvantages to incorporating sex education in schools. First, students are instructed about safe ways of having sex, ultimately serving to promote sex among young people. In other words, it validates teenage sex. Therefore, kids who weren't even thinking about sex may then consider having intercourse."

The word *intercourse* gets a few chuckles. Even Mr. Dawson cracks a smile.

Landon continues, "Another negative to sex education in schools is that the curriculum in most public schools is simply not held to a high enough standard. Many teachers are not equipped to handle the sensitive subject matter, students laugh and joke around, and the importance of the subject is minimized."

I'm pretty impressed by Landon's arguments. We go back and forth a few times before we take our seats to hear feedback and results.

"Just so you know, I'm all for sex ed," Landon says to

no one in particular as he sits back down. That gets a big laugh, especially because it comes from him, who seems like he'd be the last person on Earth willing to talk about sex. That's one of the trickiest things about being on the debate team: We often have to speak passionately on the opposite side from where our feelings really lie.

Mr. Dawson asks our teammates to give us comments and criticism, which is always helpful and sometimes surprising. It turns out everyone was really impressed that Landon made such good arguments for something he didn't personally support. Mr. Dawson announces that I am the winner by a very slight margin due to the fact that I was less emotional and more declarative than my opponent. I find it ironic that I was able to stay unemotional on the subject of sex today, the only day of my life thus far where I am actually having some real emotions on the topic.

CHAPTER SEVEN

I T'S GO TIME. School is over and I'm about to walk out to the track. I can't decide whether this is the moment I've been awaiting or dreading. Strangely, I haven't seen Luke all day today. Maybe he's not even at school. Maybe I've been duped. I mean, why would Luke Hallstrom want to go out with me, anyway? He's handsome and experienced and always surrounded by an elite group of seniors. He is adored by every girl in San Diego County. I am small and plain and unremarkable. What was I thinking, getting myself excited for a date with a guy who is so completely out of my league? It probably wasn't even Luke who was texting me last night. I'm probably getting cyberbullied by someone with mad tech skills. I'm such a fool.

As I leave the locker room and walk toward the track, I see him. He's standing with a couple of his friends. He doesn't even look in my direction. My insides collapse. This whole thing was somehow a fraud. I'm not sure how or why, but I'm absolutely certain I've gotten this all wrong. I walk slowly to the track where the other junior girls are congregated—stretching, gossiping, adjusting ponytails. I glance again toward the cluster of senior boys and confirm that Luke is acting like the same stranger he was last year. I feel so stupid for the extra effort I put into today's outfit and for telling Sloan and Danielle that I had a date with Luke. How could I even think for one minute that Luke Hallstrom could possibly be interested in me?

Chow calls us all to the starting line for a warm-up half mile. I am the first to hit stride when his whistle blows. The frustration and humiliation I feel are oddly good for endurance and speed. I take off like a shot and keep up the fast pace around the track.

"Hey," calls a voice on the track next to me. I look up to find Luke running at my side. I sent myself down a paranoid, insecure spiral for no reason at all. Is this the power of boys? Their attention or lack thereof can determine your state of mind minute to minute? Second to second? I'm not sure I have the stamina for this madness.

"Hey," I reply calmly, as though I haven't just taken a ride on the emotional roller coaster from hell.

"You still good to grab something after practice?"

"Sure." Oh my god it's real. It's really really real. I find the sheer joy makes me run even faster.

"I looked for you at lunch and didn't see you. I thought maybe you were blowing me off." Great minds think alike. It's surprising to me that while I'm trying my very hardest to play it cool, Luke is totally candid. He can plainly admit that he wondered if he was being blown off. I thought all guys acted like nothing bothers them.

"I had debate."

"Ah. Didn't know you were on debate. What'd you fight about today?"

Oh no. I have to say the word *sex* to Luke.

"The advantages of sex education in school." I'm trying to force myself to keep from blushing.

He breaks into wry little grin.

"Oh? And what did you have to say about that?" Luke asks while we keep up our pace. A significant distance grows between us and the rest of the pack.

I feel myself get shy. I may have said the word *sex,* but there's no way I can say *contraception* or *abstinence.* Once again, I can speak calmly and unemotionally in front of a room full of people on the subject of sex, but when one adorable senior boy asks me to recount my argument, I turn to Jell-O.

"Uh, I had prop. So, basically, I said that sex ed is beneficial. You know, the whole knowledge-is-power thing."

"Right. I know I'd certainly rather learn about it from a teacher than from my parents. I don't think I can handle hearing my mother use the word *penis.*"

Oh my god. Luke just said *penis.* I decide to just pretend I'm not as nervous as I feel. It occurs to me that our conversation has become much more of a priority than our run. We have slowed down to a jog and let some of our teammates pass us.

"Did your parents ever have the dreaded talk with you?" I ask as we begin our last straightaway.

"Not really. I have older siblings, so my parents probably figured I heard stuff from them. Last year, my dad bought condoms and put them in my bathroom, but we never discussed it. Like it never even happened."

"How do you know it was your dad?"

"Well, I'll tell you how I know it wasn't my mom," he says.

"How?" I ask.

"I played Little League in the third grade. My dad was out of town when the season started, and my mom couldn't bring herself to take me to buy a cup, so I had to wait until my dad came home. I missed the first game. This is not a woman who would buy condoms."

"Got it. So I guess you don't go to her for advice about girls," I say.

Luke snickers. "That's what older sisters are for."

"You're lucky. I'm an only child. But my parents think of themselves as super cool and progressive, so they're certain they serve that purpose for me."

"Do they?" he asks.

That's a very good question. I haven't really had much reason to go to my mom or dad for advice about boys, dating, sex, or condoms. But I certainly don't want to let Luke know how inexperienced I am.

"Still undetermined," I say.

• • •

Luke finishes his workout before I do. I'm running my leg of the relay when I see him throw on a sweatshirt and toss his water cup in the trash. Then he sits, watching my team finish our practice. I think I run faster when he's watching. It's cool the way he doesn't pretend to be busy doing something else, like checking his phone or talking to his friends. He's not trying to hide that he's waiting around for me. When I'm finally finished, he tells me to grab my stuff and meet him in the student parking lot.

I go into the locker room to get my backpack and duffle bag. I splash some cold water on my face, shake my hair out of the ponytail, and throw my hoodie on over my running clothes. I don't want to leave him waiting, but I don't want to sprint out the door too eagerly, either. It's funny to have to think about all this stuff: Hair up or down? School clothes or workout clothes? Hurry or stall? I never realized how simple life was without strategizing for a boy.

I walk to the parking lot and Luke is leaning against his black Jeep. He looks really cute in his gray Boston College sweatshirt and with his messy hair. He takes my bag and backpack, throws them in the back seat, and opens the door for me. I'm starting to think this might be a real date. During the five-minute drive to the juice place he turns down the music so that we can talk. He asks me questions about school and where I want to go to college. We talk about Stanford and East Coast versus West Coast schools.

"I think it was just always a given that my siblings and I would go to college back east. My parents are both from Massachusetts, and when I graduate in June, they're moving back. That way they'll be close when I'm in college."

"Let me guess," I say, giving a nod to his sweatshirt, "Boston College?"

"Yep. Early decision. Got the news before we left for Cabo. They have a great track team. I'm really excited."

At the juice place, we step up to the counter. Luke asks me what I'd like. I speak directly to the guy working there.

"I'll have a small Peachy Keen, please."

Luke laughs out loud. He does this adorable thing with his tongue when he laughs—it sticks out ever so slightly onto his bottom lip. I am thoroughly captivated by how cute he looks when he laughs that it takes me a moment to realize I have no idea what he's laughing at. Did I do something wrong?

"What?" I want to know.

"Nothing."

"No. What's so funny?"

"You just sound like a little girl ordering that. It's cute."

He just called me cute. I'm having the best time.

"Oh, and you have some macho smoothie order? Like Big Banana Man?"

If only I had anticipated how those words would sound. First Luke said *penis,* and then I said *big banana man.* I feel my face turn crimson. Luke raises his eyebrows.

"Well, I won't argue . . ."

We laugh so hard we can barely finish ordering. The guy at the cash register looks at us like we're crazy. When I try to pay, Luke shuts me down, telling me that maybe he'll let me get it next time. His saying that there will be a next time is just about the greatest news ever.

We take our smoothies and sit outside. We keep laughing about Peachy Keen and Big Banana Man. When the laughter subsides, we end up having a real conversation. He asks me about my family, and I'm entirely at ease talking about my parents' current situation. He's compassionate, telling me that his aunt and uncle got divorced and they were so mean and awful to each other during and after, which made it really rough on his cousins.

"You're lucky your mom and dad are such good friends," he reassures me.

"Yeah, I guess. It just seems to me that if they still like each other so much, why don't they just stay together?"

"Well, did they tell you why they're getting divorced?" he asks, with genuine interest.

"They said the magic is gone."

"That sucks," he says.

I shrug. He notices and seems curious.

"What's that about? You don't care if they're hot for each other or not?" He smiles and patiently waits for me to respond.

"They're fortysomething. How long do they really expect to see fireworks?"

"Point taken." Luke leans toward me, still smiling. "Question for you: Have you ever been in love?"

Whoa! That came out of nowhere. He's looking deep into my eyes, like he can see my soul. I have no choice but to answer honestly.

"No. I haven't," I say.

"Well, it's not like I'm an expert on love and marriage," he says, "but I can bet it's a bummer to live with someone you're not in love with."

"Right." I still can't look away from his chocolate-brown eyes.

"I mean, I don't know about you," he says, "but I wouldn't want that kind of marriage. Seems like it would pretty much suck."

How is he so comfortable talking about such intimate things? I honestly never would have guessed that boys even thought about relationships, love, marriage, and the rest of it. And never, in a million years, did I think they would want to *talk* about it.

"Interesting," I say. Wait, did I just say that out loud?

"What's interesting?" he asks.

"Just that we're having this conversation. I don't usually talk to people about this kind of thing."

"Me neither," he says.

"You're so accepting."

"Well, we've had a bunch of talks about relationship stuff in my family," he says. "My brother Jackson came out when he was a senior in high school. I was in eighth grade. Jackson was always my hero. Still is."

"Wow," I say. "That's a big deal."

"It was then. Not so much anymore. It's pretty simple, actually. If he's happy, I'm happy."

"And is he happy?" I ask.

Luke takes the last sip of his smoothie and I can hear his straw scraping along the bottom of the cup.

"Yeah. He has a boyfriend. Brady. They're hilarious."

Luke is unbelievably easy to talk to. There are no lulls in our conversation, and I don't feel like I have to come up with things to say. In addition to parents, we cover high school, track, college, music, and movies. We laugh about *Family Guy* episodes and failed science projects. He plays me his favorite Bob Marley song on his phone and I show him the scar on my hand from my attempt to bake a chocolate soufflé. I ask him about the braided leather bracelet and he tells me he bought it in Mexico and that he hasn't taken it off since the trip.

"You're different," he says to me, a total non sequitur. Here we go—he has noticed that I'm nerdy and slightly awkward and not like the giggly, flirty girls he's used to dating.

"How am I different?" I ask, bracing myself for what's to come.

"You're smart, and you have a lot to say. I really like talking to you."

"Well, thanks," I say. "I like talking to you, too. You're wise. Like an old soul."

"That's so funny. My mom always calls me that," he says.

He offers to drive me home, and when we finally get into his car, I hear my phone, from deep in my backpack, blasting the "Mamma Mia" ringtone, letting me know it's none other than my mom. She's used to returning from work and finding me safe at home after track, diligently doing my homework. I assure her that I'm not in somebody's trunk and that I'll be home shortly.

"Can I see that?" Luke reaches for my phone.

I hand it to him. He starts pressing buttons.

"What are you doing?"

"I'm putting in all my information so you have no excuse not to call or text me."

"I see. And when am I supposed to be doing all this calling and texting?" There's that smile again, plastered across my face

"Whenever."

The drive home is much too quick. It's the first time I've ever wished to be caught in a horrible traffic jam. We pull up in front of my house and I am at a complete loss as to what I'm supposed to do next.

"Thanks again for my Peachy Keen. You should have let me pay for myself." I reach for the door handle, but he stops me with a hand on my arm.

"Can I ask you a question?" Once again, he looks right through me.

"Of course," I say.

"Is this your first date?" Now I'm back in the same place I was before: staring into his eyes, feeling frighteningly exposed. It's one thing to admit I've never been in love, but do I really have to confess that I've never been on a date before?

"Well, is this an official date?" I'm glad to have the opportunity to pose the question I've been asking myself all day.

"That depends. What makes a date official?" His whole face seems to be smiling.

I'm back in the hot seat. What am I supposed to say to that? I hesitate, more unsure of my words than ever before. "Um, I guess an official date is an occasion where two people agree to a plan—"

He interrupts me, "Any two people?"

"What do you mean?"

"I mean, it's usually two people who like each other, right?" he asks.

"Well, yes, but maybe they don't know how the other one feels."

"True."

I decide to turn it around, put him on the spot for once. "So, Big Banana Man, how would you define a date?"

"Hmm." He pauses for a moment and appears to be giving it a lot of thought. "I think it's all about the kiss."

Holy moly. My heartbeat is back to its circus act. "The kiss?"

"If there's a kiss, it's probably a date."

I have no words. What could I possibly say to that? Then I realize I need no words because he's leaning toward me. Slowly, slowly his face nears mine. Those full lips are slightly parted. Here we go.

I close my eyes and lean in. Our lips touch, softly at first, with a little peck. Then we kiss again, and this time we stay pressed together a little longer. He opens his mouth slightly, and I follow. I have never done this before and am terrified that I'm doing it wrong. I'm really not sure what to do with my tongue. His tongue ever so gently finds mine, and our two tongues do a little dance. I am lost in him, in his soft lips, his smooth tongue, his yummy smell. I quickly pick up his rhythm, and it's much easier than I thought it would be. I could do this all day.

Finally, we pull apart and open our eyes. Instinctively, I let out a big, audible sigh. He chuckles.

"Guess this was a date," I say. I lean forward, give him one little peck on those delicious lips, grab my stuff, and float into my house.

CHAPTER EIGHT

I'M NOT SURE how I got from Luke's car to my front porch. I really never felt my feet touch the ground. I guess that's what people mean when they say they're walking on air. I have the same peaceful, buoyant sensation when I walk through the front door, but it all comes to a crashing halt when I see my mom sitting on the striped love seat in the living room, a book in her lap.

"Hello there."

I've been awakened from my reverie.

"Hi."

"Who was that?" she asks, her voice light and curious.

"Who was what?" It's not my intention to keep secrets from my mom; I just don't quite know what to tell her about Luke. Moms tend to make something out of nothing, and this might still be nothing. For all I know, Luke has a date with someone else for dinner tonight. The general perception is that he's very experienced. I don't want my mom to think I have a boyfriend.

"The boy you were kissing in the Jeep." She says it

without any motherly judgment or pointed accusations. She has a little gleam in her eye, almost as if she's excited about it as well.

"Oh. Him." I suppose if I wanted to keep it under wraps, I probably shouldn't have kissed him directly in front of my house under the street lamp.

Mom smiles. "Yeah, him."

I smile back. It's difficult not to. "Luke Hallstrom."

"The cute one from track?" Funny that my mom knows exactly who he is. Even funnier that she thinks he's cute. Maybe we have the same taste, or maybe Luke is just cute—objectively and empirically speaking.

"That would be the one." I can't stop smiling.

"You look happy," she says.

"I think I am," I admit.

"Tell me."

Forget the idea about pretending that this might be nothing. I end up telling my mom the whole story, starting with the airplane and ending where she caught up with us in front of the house. Obviously, I leave out the details about his soft lips and heavenly scent. It feels so good to share with the one person in the world I know is rooting for me and only me. I don't have to put any kind of spin on it or act like I'm not that into him. I'm utterly and absolutely on cloud nine, and my mother is right there with me.

It finally occurs to me that my mom and I have had

this time to talk, and I haven't been met with the pretend picture-perfect family dinner.

"Where's Dad?"

Her face falls a little. She pauses.

"He's out."

So much for the grand gestures to keep things as normal as possible.

"When will he be home?"

The pause is even longer this time. "I'm not sure he's coming home tonight."

I just went from walking on air to hitting the ground . . . hard.

"Oh."

"I think he's going to dinner and a movie with Uncle Ed. He might just sleep at Ed's."

She looks intently at me, searching for signs of emotional tremors, tears, despondency. I feel surprised. Sad, but not sad enough to cry. Maybe it's good that there was some time between the initial news and the first real signs of separation. Maybe it's good that I had a few days to wonder when it's going kick in. Maybe I'm sort of ready. Maybe not.

"You okay?" she asks.

"Yeah," I say. I think I'm telling the truth. It's nearly impossible to tell with so many emotions coursing through my veins. I've always been the kid who had no answer when someone asked, "What's new?" Things have been stable and consistent for as long as I can remember. I've always lived in San Diego; in fact, I've lived in the same house since I was six. My parents have had the same jobs for too many years to count. My friends have remained largely the same. I've never been in love. And besides some forgettable girl drama in seventh grade, I've had very few real disappointments in my life. My grandmother did pass away two years ago. But she lived in Virginia and was sick for many years, so by the time she died, we were all emotionally prepared.

Now, in the last twenty minutes, I have experienced the high of having my first kiss with a beautiful boy, and the low of returning home to discover that my father is *out*. The questions start spinning through my brain. Is he really with Uncle Ed? Is there a woman involved? Are he and Ed on a double date?

I hear my cell phone ringing from my bag on the floor where I dropped my stuff. I can't imagine anyone I want to talk to right now. Even Luke.

"You don't want to get that?" Mom asks.

"Not really," I say.

"Might be Dad." Mom clearly wants me to check my phone, so I do. It's Dad.

"It's him," I say.

"I think you should talk to him," she says, taking her book and walking out of the room to give me some privacy.

"Hi, Dad," I say, answering the phone.

"Hi, kid." His voice is a little too chipper. Is that because he's trying to keep our conversation light and happy? Or because he's thrilled to be out . . . most likely on a date . . . with a woman . . . who isn't my mother?

"You home yet?" he wants to know.

"Yep."

His voice loses its perkiness. "I won't be home tonight."

"Okay."

"I'm sorry I'll miss dinner with you. I wanted to talk to you this morning, but there wasn't time. I love you so much." He sounds sincere and slightly more gloomy than when I answered the phone. I know he loves me. I know our family dinners are important to him. Maybe he is suffering, too.

"I love you, too, Dad."

"Can we go out to dinner Friday night?"

"Sure," I say.

"Great." He seems genuinely happy. "Anywhere you want."

"Sushi?" Sushi isn't my dad's favorite, but he knows I love it, so every once in a while he surrenders and comes with us to our favorite little Japanese restaurant in La Jolla.

"All the sushi you can eat," he promises. "Love you, kid."

"Love you back." I hang up the phone and walk into

the kitchen, where my mom is sitting at the table pouring honey into two mugs of chamomile tea. I join her and add a little extra honey to mine.

"We're going to get through this," she assures me. Her eyes look a little misty.

"I know." And I do know. But does she?

When they first told me the news, I only thought of myself. I wondered how this change would affect me, my life, my schedule, my junior year. But hearing my dad's voice tonight and seeing my mom's sad eyes makes me acutely aware that I'm not the only one hurting. I am reminded of Luke's words, and I realize that I need to think of my parents as people, human beings with feelings. Now I'm looking at my mom and I see a woman dealing with real sadness. And yet, I can tell that her primary concern is that I'm okay. I think I'm okay. I hope she is.

CHAPTER NINE

I NEVER THOUGHT I'd be this psyched to be in the locker room, changing for a workout. The school day was endless. Each period crawled by while I watched the clock, willing the minutes to pass so I could walk through the hallway to the next class, hoping for a chance encounter with Luke. I saw him from afar at lunch. I was in line buying a blueberry muffin while he was entering the cafeteria with his friend Miles. We smiled at each other as though we shared the best secret ever. Just that smile, that connection across lunch trays, hairnets, and rowdy students, was all I needed to survive until three o'clock. It was a reminder that I'm not dreaming or embellishing or out of my mind.

I have not discussed any of the Luke stuff with Brett. I want to avoid the subject with him, so I told Brett I didn't need a ride to school this morning. I know Brett well enough to predict that he won't be in favor of whatever it is that is brewing between me and Luke. Brett tends to be extremely critical. He often makes derogatory, snarky comments about sporty boys or vapid girls. He makes me laugh even though he's sometimes a little harsh. But I don't want to hear anything negative about Luke. I'll tell Brett about Luke when I need to, when and if it's clear there's really something to tell. A smoothie and a kiss is not a big enough something.

Naturally, Sloan and Danielle wanted to know every gory detail about the smoothie date. They wanted to Face-Time last night, but I wasn't much in the mood to talk given the whole situation with my parents. The girls bombarded me this morning in the parking lot after my mom dropped me off. I want to share with them, but I'm afraid of jinxing whatever is developing with Luke. I still worry that it will just evaporate like it never happened at all.

What if Sloan opens her mouth about it, and it gets back to Luke that I'm yammering on as if we have the greatest romance since Marge and Homer Simpson? That would be mortifying. So I merely said we went to get smoothies and hung out, and then he drove me home. I admitted that I think he's really cute, but that's basically all I would confess. I think they can tell I'm keeping things under wraps. Danielle backed off, but Sloan seemed annoyed.

As best friends, we typically know what the others are doing every minute of every day. If we're not together, we're in touch on our phones, or we're aware of one another's schedules. They know when I'm at track, Sloan and I know when Danielle is at dance, and everyone knows that Sloan used to stop at Starbucks every day before school until she made a New Year's resolution to cut out caffeine.

I'm almost ready to head out to the track. I actually use a brush to pull my hair into a smooth ponytail. This is the first time in my life I've ever brought a hairbrush to school, including picture days. What's next? Mascara? Nail polish? Lucy Koch, another junior girl on the track team, is arranging her breasts in her skin-tight tank top. I watch to see if she's going to cover up with a T-shirt. Nope. Off she goes, out the door, with her boobs on display. I look back in the mirror. In my mind's eye, I still look like a twelve-year-old girl. I wonder what Luke sees when he looks at me.

When I get to the track, Luke is at the long jump pit with Miles and a senior girl named Ella. Ella is one of the best athletes at school. She's the number one seed on girls' varsity tennis and the fastest sprinter on the track team. She also happens to have the most awesome body in school. Brett says her ass is perfection. Ella leans on Luke's shoulder as she pulls one heel to her butt in a quad stretch. Luke feigns like he's going to walk away, which, just as he seems to have planned, makes Ella lose her balance. He catches her arm to keep her from falling and they both laugh. It's a blatantly flirtatious encounter, and witnessing it makes me feel uncomfortable, and a little stupid. Why would I think Luke and I could be something when he has opportunities like these at every turn?

I start my warm-up run and get crazy nervous when I near the pit. Ella is gone and Luke waits while Miles jumps. The butterflies in my stomach are doing backflips. I haven't said a word to Luke since I got out of his car last night. Do I look at him? Do I merely stare straight ahead? He hasn't noticed me yet, because his back is to me as he prepares to jump. I am approaching him as he takes his five long strides and hits the jumping board. He shoots his chest out, looks to the sky, and throws his arms behind his body. He lands in the sand with his legs in front of him and turns around just as I'm approaching.

"Go, Peachy Keen," Luke calls out.

I almost laugh out loud. I love not only that he's cheering me on, but that he has a funny nickname for me and he's not embarrassed to use it in front of his buddy.

"Very funny," I manage to say as I keep charging around the track, trying to keep from smiling.

On several occasions during the rest of the workout, Luke and I glance each other's way and smirk. I see him doing high jumps from where I work on wind sprints. I never would have imagined that I could have so much fun with a guy from clear across a football field. It's a bummer when practice ends; the two hours have gone by much too quickly. People grab their backpacks and file off the track. I start to leave, but Luke motions for me to join him by the high jump. I refrain from racing over there at warp speed.

"Nice hurdles."

"Thanks," I say. "Good job on high jump. I'll never figure out how you get that height."

"Come here, I'll show you."

I climb onto the mat. He leans in really close to me. Oh my god, is he going to kiss me right here in the middle of the field in the light of the waning sun? His eyes are really close to my eyes and his lips are really close to my lips. I'm not sure how I feel about this.

"Hi," he whispers.

"Hi," I say back softly and nervously.

"Let me show you the Fosbury Flop." He's still whispering.

What on Earth is he talking about? I keep staring at him, wondering what is happening here. He bursts out laughing, and this time his tongue is in full view, pink and smooth. Finally he speaks in a normal voice.

"The Fosbury Flop is a high jump technique where you arch over the bar to lower your center of gravity."

For the next half-hour, Luke teaches me how to high jump. He lowers the bar to four feet, which is a whole lot lower than the height he clears. He teaches me the ten steps of the approach, in the shape of a *J*. He makes fun of my *J*, calling it lowercase, which makes me laugh. He then demonstrates the takeoff and grabs my hands to show me that they should move forward and up. The real fun starts when it's time to learn how to move in the air. Having the boy I like teach me how to thrust my hips and tilt my head back is an experience like no other. Who knew the high jump could be so exciting?

Afterward, Luke drives me home, and again, we're sitting in his car in front of my house.

"Can we do something Friday night?" he wants to know. Wow, that sounds like a real date, not one that needs a kiss to qualify it. Naturally, my first instinct is to scream *YES YES YES!* at the top of my lungs, but then I remember my dad and how we made a plan to have sushi Friday night.

"I can't," I say.

I can see him try to cover his surprise. "Hot date with a faster runner?"

"Not quite. My father." I tell him how things with the separation are escalating and that it's starting to feel real. He is so understanding, which makes me like him more, if that's even possible.

"How about you save room for dessert and call me when you get home from sushi?" he says.

"That sounds good," I say.

He leans in and gives me a soft kiss on the lips. Nothing sexy or smoochy; just soft, sweet, and delicious. It feels like just the right kind of kiss to get from a boy after you've talked about your parents' divorce. The irony of the timing is not lost on me: I'm starting up a romance while my parents' romance, the only real reference point I have for relationships, is dissolving.

CHAPTER TEN

I T'S FRIDAY EVENING and there's a lot in store for me tonight—dinner with my dad, which is sure to be weird because he's going to want to talk about everything. My dad is all about communication. He always digs deep, wanting to know my feelings, reactions, and opinions about every challenge I face. He's not going to let me get away with one-word answers or *I don't know* responses to his questions. I guess when you have only one kid, you put all your eggs in that basket and you want to make sure you're doing it right. My parents have always rejected the term *only child* in favor of *exclusive child,* which I find ridiculous, yet sort of endearing.

And then round two will be dessert with Luke. Where will we go? How late will we stay out? Should I pay for dessert since he bought smoothies? Do I invite him to come into the house when he drops me off? It might be time to open up to Danielle and Sloan, at least so I can get answers to these logistical questions. These are things girls share with their best friends, and I desperately want to tell someone how excited I am. Besides, I could really use some coaching.

When I think about clothing choices for the evening, I almost laugh, picturing myself dressed in a frumpy librarian frock for dinner with Dad and then ducking into a phone booth à la Superman, emerging moments later in a sexy black number for my dessert date with Luke. But the truth is, I don't own a sexy black number. I decide that jeans, boots, and a sweater will work for both parts of my double-header.

Now, sitting at the far end of the sushi bar at Sushi Mori, I stare at my dad, and I swear he looks different. I'm not sure I'd say he looks happier, but he seems lighter, brighter, more easygoing. It could be that he's making every effort to make sure we have a good time, but I really think it's more than that. I need to try not to take it personally that maybe he's enjoying his freedom. But how can I not take that personally?

We gloss over the usual topics: the weather, school, track, friends, his work, and the Lakers (it's tragic that there's no NBA team in San Diego). When our waitress comes to take our order, Dad motions to me and tells me not to hold back, so I really go for it and order all my favorite rolls. I figure at some point this dinner is going to get strange, so I might as well have plenty of yellowtail, salmon, and albacore to ease the discomfort.

As soon as the waitress takes one step away from our table, Dad grabs my hand.

"I miss being at home with you," he says. Here we go.

"I miss you, too," I say. I get that lump in my throat and blink about a hundred times, hoping the tears will stay inside my eyes instead of rolling onto my cheeks.

"I want us to be able to talk about this. I know you probably have a lot of questions, and you're old enough to know the answers. I'm here to indulge your curiosities." That is so Dad.

"Were you on a date the other night?" I ask.

He does not hesitate before responding: "No." I practically crumble in relief. "But I do have a sort-of date tomorrow night." Blink blink blink.

"Who is she?" I hear the edge and judgment in my voice. I can't help it. My dad hears it as well, loud and clear. His tone is calming, a little defensive.

"I've never even met her, so before you go thinking anything improper happened, I'll tell you right now that you would be wrong. This separation is a mutual decision between Mom and me. No one has come between us."

I sigh. I remove all sharpness and criticism from my tone.

"Who is she?" I ask with exaggerated cheerfulness and a plastic grin.

"Very funny. She's a lawyer in Uncle Ed's office. She's recently separated as well, and Ed thought we could be friends. We had one phone conversation, and I'm meeting her for a drink tomorrow. Not even dinner."

I bust out my phone.

"What's her name? Let's look her up on Facebook."

"That is not happening. I'm not going to cyberstalk her. I'm going to get to know her the old-fashioned way."

"You're no fun," I say. This time my smile is genuine.

"I'm sure it must be strange for you to know I will be on a date. You're the one who should be dating, right?" He leans in ever so subtly, his smirk giving him away.

"Mom told you." I should have known. Those two tell each other everything. If I so much as sneeze in front of Mom, Dad will hear all about it.

"Yeah. But if there's anything more you want to share, I'd love to know," he says.

"There's nothing to tell. He drove me home from practice a couple of times. He's nice." That seems to be all the information Dad needs. He's clearly not looking for graphic details.

"I guess we're all going through some changes," he says softly.

"Guess so." Just the thought of Luke puts me in a better mood.

The food comes and we actually end up having a really good time together. I laugh watching my dad pretend to enjoy the yellowtail when I know he'd much rather be scarfing down a burger and fries. He tells me that he's renting a little apartment near the beach in Del Mar and he wants me to come see it. I'll have my own room there, and we can decorate it however I'd like. I promise that next week, when he gets back from his trip to Washington and Oregon, I'll spend the night at his new place.

After Dad pays the bill, we head outside and start walking toward the car.

"Want to get some ice cream?" Dad wants to know.

"No thanks." I feel bad. Clearly he wants our time together to continue.

He does a whole dramatic heartbroken routine.

"What? No ice cream? Are you saying I have to eat ice cream all by myself?" he asks with mock tears.

"Um . . . well . . . the thing is . . ."

Now he's ultra-curious. He stops walking and looks at me questioningly.

"What's the thing, Janey dear?"

"I'm supposed to meet Luke for dessert," I say apologetically.

"What, are you speed dating or something?"

"No. It's just that he wanted to do something tonight, but I was seeing you for dinner, so he asked if we could have dessert. Are you angry?"

Again, he does a big performance of a crushed heart and crocodile tears.

"Of course I'm not angry. Let's get you home so you can have your dessert and still get to bed at a decent time. ALONE!"

"DAD!" I can't believe him. My dad's always been really open and easy to talk to. However, I am completely unprepared for references to me and actual sexual activity with an actual boy.

I text Luke when we leave the restaurant, and when Dad pulls up to my house (I guess I can't say *our* house anymore), Luke's Jeep is parked at the curb and he's sitting on our front porch. He looks so cute, I can feel my insides quicken to the point where I have to take a deep breath. Dad notices my reaction, but thankfully says nothing, which must be excruciating for him. We get out of the car and Luke walks toward us. We all meet halfway up the walkway.

I'm so uncomfortable having Luke and my dad approaching each other, I wish I could slip into one of the cracks in the pavement.

"Dad, this is Luke. Luke, my dad."

"Nice to meet you, Mr. King." Luke extends his hand and shakes my dad's. Dad seems impressed; he's always been a sucker for a kid with good manners.

"Pleasure to meet you, too, Luke. Don't keep her out too late." Guess he had to get some fatherly words in there. He squeezes me tight and gives me a kiss on the forehead before slowly making his way back to his car.

When we're officially alone, Luke and I look at each other. He leans down and kisses me sweetly on the lips.

"That should answer any questions about whether this is a date," he assures me.

"I'm so glad you cleared that up." I can tell this is going to be the best dessert *ever.*

Luke takes me to a little place that has authentic gelato. He holds my hand as we walk from the car into Gelateria Frizzante. I love how he isn't self-conscious about who might see us and what they might think. If not for his confidence, I would be dying inside, wondering if someone we knew from school was nearby and how the word would spread. I can't help but think people would speculate about why the hunky Luke Hallstrom is with the no-body Janey King.

We walk up to the counter and gaze at all the gelato options. There are too many flavors to choose just one.

"Guess it would be easier if they had Peachy Keen," Luke teases me.

"I will never live that down, will I?"

"Aw, come on, it's adorable," he says. "I've got this; you go grab a table."

I go find a little table in the corner and wait. A few minutes later, Luke walks toward me weighed down by eight or nine cups of gelato.

"Hungry?" I ask him with a snicker.

"You need to try all of these. That way, next time we come, you'll know exactly what you want." OMG, we're coming back again. Yay.

The little table is barely big enough to hold everything he bought. Luke arranges the cups strategically, making our table deliciously crowded. An older couple nearby watches curiously. Luke takes two spoons and a bunch of napkins out of his pockets.

"Choose your weapon," he says.

I grab a spoon and dig right into the chocolate hazel-nut. It's heavenly. Then I try the piña colada, followed by the blood orange, which is Luke's favorite by far.

Luke asks about my dinner with my dad. I tell him everything, a little floored by my own ability to be so candid with him. He listens attentively, looking at me while I talk, as if he really wants to know what's going on.

"I'm sorry you're going through this. You know I'm here if you ever want to talk about it."

"Thanks. That's so nice. I guess I always thought we'd be a family forever."

Luke reaches across the table and puts his hand on mine.

"What's your family like?" I ask, trying lamely to take the spotlight off my sad broken home.

"They're true Bostonians. My parents met in college when my dad was at Harvard and my mom was at BU. They were both on the T late one night and started talking. They got off the train together and ended up walking around and talking until the sun came up. The rest is history."

"That's pretty romantic," I say, wishing my parents had a cool story like that, as opposed to the boring one where they had mutual friends and met at some Memorial Day barbecue. Where's the romance in that?

"Yeah. They really love Boston. And each other, I guess. They've talked about moving back to the East Coast since I can remember."

"And now it's happening?" I ask.

"Yep, they have a realtor looking for houses there," he says. "And they're getting ready to sell our house here. The plan is that we're all packing up and moving east right after graduation."

"Do you think you'll spend a lot of time with them while you're at school?"

"When my brother left, I swear they wanted to move right on campus with him and make sure he ate three square meals a day. But, you know, I'm the third kid, so they're practically counting the minutes until they have their freedom."

"Hey, they're moving to Boston to be close to their kids. So they aren't looking for too much freedom," I say.

"True. They're all about family. They'll probably figure out a way to make us all come for Sunday-night dinners," he says.

"Maybe you'll be very happy to have a home-cooked meal," I say.

My mind starts racing ahead to the fall. Luke and his entire family will be in Massachusetts. He'll have no reason to come back here. No visits over Thanksgiving or winter breaks. No long weekends in San Diego pretending he's visiting his parents, but really here to see me. I take a huge bite of chocolate banana nut crunch and make myself focus on the here and now.

Luke and I close the place down. We don't even come close to finishing all the gelato he bought. It was an absurd amount of food in the first place. Now it's just melted pools of sugar and cream. When the guy from behind the counter starts putting chairs up on the tables and mopping the floors, we know it's our cue to leave.

Back at my house, Luke walks me to the door. We've held hands all the way home, but he hasn't kissed me since that sweet little peck on the lips right after my dad drove away. I'm wondering if I'm supposed to ask him to come in the house. If he does, what would we do? Where would we go? I couldn't take him to my room. Would we watch TV? Would we hang out with my mom? It all seems so horribly awkward.

"I guess I should go," he says.

"Okay," I say, hoping he'll never ever leave.

"That was fun," he says. "You're fun." He leans toward me. His hands reach up and push my hair gently away from my face. His eyes stay on my eyes until his lips touch mine. My eyes close as he opens his mouth and his tongue finds mine. I feel myself grow weak and I lean back on the front door to keep from falling. I don't know what to do with my hands and, as a result, my arms hang limply and lamely at my sides.

He leans into me, his body up against mine. It feels like he's protecting and guarding me. For the next several minutes, he kisses me. Our lips never part. His hands stay in my hair while his tongue continues to play with mine. It's both gentle and sexy at the same time. I could do this forever and ever. It's like time stands still and nothing else matters. Not my parents' divorce, nor debate, nor track, nor my friends. I am undeniably lost in Luke and only Luke. Waves of weakness and strength crash into each other throughout my body. Is this what falling in love feels like? This euphoria? This sense of being protected and adored? If so, then sign me up, because nothing has ever felt so good.

CHAPTER ELEVEN

Y ALARM GOES OFF Saturday morning
at seven and I can't pull myself out from
under my covers. I have a debate at Kearny
High School and Brett is picking me up in twenty minutes. This morning is much different from recent mornings when I woke early for school, bounded out of bed,
and launched right into a wardrobe and grooming routine unlike ever before. Knowing I won't be seeing Luke
today takes away all my motivation to rise and shine.

I'm ready when Brett arrives. And by ready, I mean
that I'm dressed, my teeth are brushed, and my debate
notes are neatly assembled in my binder. But I don't feel
as ready as I have for previous tournaments. I usually do
nothing the night before a debate but prepare notes, go
over arguments, and practice closing statements. Last night
I was eating gelato and making out on my doorstep until
past midnight. I think I'm starting to lose focus.

"What did you do last night?" Brett wants to know. "I
thought we could FaceTime and practice for today."

"Dinner with my dad." I hear the words leave my lips and I realize that I sound like a child of divorce. I hate the way it sounds.

"That's it?" He knows me so well.

"What do you mean?" I ask.

"I mean I was trying you at ten thirty. You and your dad have a late night on the town?"

Am I supposed to tell Brett where I was and what I was doing? I'm not sure where to draw the line between honesty and privacy.

"Came home and went to bed." Wow, I just lied to Brett.

He seems suspicious, but he lets it go. Guys are so much simpler than girls.

We arrive at the high school and enter the auditorium to register. These mornings are always frantic. Team members are keyed up, going over their outlines, making last-minute notes, and checking their computers for new findings that support their arguments. Those who are unprepared (I never knew what that felt like until today) ask to see their teammates' research to scan for missing information. I sit down at a table and try to lock in on my outlines for a quick cram session before round one begins. I should be thinking about immigration, peer pressure, and gun control, but instead I'm thinking about gelato, Peachy Keen smoothies, and Luke's soft, sweet lips. This debate is going to go horribly wrong, and yet I'm fighting to keep a smile from creeping across my face.

The first round of the tournament, we are debating the topic *The negative effects of peer pressure outweigh the positive ones.* I am the first speaker for the proposition side. I stand up and wait for the judge to signal that he's ready to begin.

"Our peers have a huge influence on us. We are impacted in ways that make us adopt their thinking, their behavior, and their lifestyle, which is, in effect, the definition of peer pressure. It can be argued that there are indeed positive effects of peer pressure. But, Judge, the negative impact is far weightier. Teenagers are susceptible to both negative and positive peer pressure, but in my arguments, I will explain and prove that the negative effects far outweigh the positive."

I'm not in my groove. I don't feel rehearsed or proficient, the way I usually do. I am glancing at my notes, instead of my usual tactic: laser vision directed at the judge. I'm getting sweaty, and my hands are shaking more than usual.

"Teenagers are simply not experienced or mature enough to differentiate between good and bad. They need to be taught the difference. They need to be educated about and protected against the negative and harmful effects of peer pressure. The solution, Judge, is not in isolating these adolescents from peers, but instead in teaching them to make good choices now and throughout their lives."

Somehow, I fill up the full five-minute time allotted

and finish my opening statements. I'm so glad it's over, but I'm supremely unhappy with my performance. Brett totally steps up. He reinforces my arguments, adding new information and examples. He delivers them with a hammer and takes our opponents down in refuting all of their points. The rest of the day goes similarly. Our team does well, fifth place, but I don't get my usual high speaker points, and I walk away without a personal trophy.

Brett and I are quiet for the first ten minutes of the ride home. Finally, he can't stand it.

"What's going on with you?" he demands.

"What do you mean?"

"Janey, how long have we known each other? You think I can't tell when something's up?"

"Everything's fine. Really." The words just come out. I ask myself why I'm lying to Brett. Why I don't just tell him: *I went out with Luke Hallstrom, I am beyond crazy for him, I spent last night kissing him instead of preparing for this tournament, and my priorities are entirely out of whack.* I am going to have to come clean to Brett sooner rather than later. I know he'd like to be in a relationship with someone, and I'm afraid he'll feel abandoned. Brett and I are sort of a team. We have each other when we have no one else. The problem is that Brett has unrealistic expectations about the girl he's waiting for: She has to be a genius, have a body that stops traffic, and of course find him one hundred percent irresistible.

Also, Brett always says the senior sporty boys are

douchey. He never specifically called Luke a douche, but it's clear he thinks that group of guys has no substance. The truth is that Brett has never even had a conversation with any of them.

I ponder all of this in my head and contemplate coming clean, but I've already denied being distracted, and now it's too late for honesty. We downshift into talk about Danielle and Charlie. Brett wants to know all the places they've had sex. I try not to betray Danielle's confidence, so I only share the widely known information.

"Let's see. I know they did it in her dad's car while it was in the garage and her parents were watching a movie upstairs."

"Yeah, I know that one. Where else?"

I feel I have to give him something to make up for the fact that I've withheld details about myself.

"They did it after school in the multipurpose room."

"No way! How'd they manage that?" he asks.

"Most of the teachers had left for the day. The door was unlocked, so they snuck in, locked the door, and went to town on a table," I say.

"Nasty! That room will never be the same."

"I know, right?"

CHAPTER TWELVE

SUNDAY MORNING. So nice to sleep late without having to worry about rushing to school or a debate tournament. After blinking the sleep from my eyes, I roll over and check my phone. The first thing I see is that it's 10:50 a.m. The second thing I notice is that I have texts from Danielle and Sloan, but none from Luke. No contact from him since Friday night. Is that bad? What does that mean? I wonder what he did Saturday night. Is it even any of my business? Do I wait for him to text me? I'm still not sure how this is supposed to work.

The texts from Danielle and Sloan tell me to get my butt out of bed and meet them in La Jolla for coffee and shopping. I brush my teeth and throw on some sweats. My mom has left a note under my door: *Went to the farmers' market, let me know if you want anything. Tacos tonight?*

When I walk up to the Living Room, Danielle and Sloan are sitting outside sipping decaf soy lattes. Mine is waiting for me. A giant cinnamon roll sits in the center of the table, three forks stabbed into its gooey frosting.

Danielle looks great, beautifully put together in skinny jeans, flats, and a cashmere sweater. Sloan, on the other hand, looks like she's been hit by a truck. She's wearing big dark sunglasses, a sure sign that she's not wearing any makeup. Her oversized La Jolla High sweatshirt and leggings could easily have served as last night's pajamas.

"Rough night?" I ask Sloan as I sit down.

"Ugh," she grunts in response.

"What did you do?" I ask.

"I went with my sister to the party on Pearl. I heard it was going to be fun. It was nuts. So many hot guys."

"Just how many are we talking about?" I ask with interest.

"Well, two worth mentioning."

Danielle nearly chokes on her foam. "E.B., you hooked up with two guys last night?"

"I did," Sloan says.

"Details," I prod.

"The first guy, I think his name is Tony . . ." Danielle and I laugh out loud because Sloan is uncertain of the name of the guy she hooked up with a mere twelve hours ago.

"Go on."

"He was so freakin' cute. We were hanging out, but his friends wanted to leave, so I walked him out and we just started kissing like crazy. Then he left. So what was I supposed to do, mourn him? No way. I started dancing and this hot guy with a nose ring was dancing near me.

We kept looking at each other until we were dancing together, and the next thing you know, DFMO."

"What is DFMO?" Danielle asks.

Sloan sighs as if it's the most obvious thing, "Dance Floor Make-Out."

"How does that even happen?" I still feel like a stranger in these waters.

"It just happens," Sloan says.

"It happens to E.B.," Danielle adds.

"So, we hung out till three a.m. When I'm with my sister, my parents don't sweat the curfew. Now I'm really wishing this wasn't decaf," she says as she lifts her drink to take a sip.

"Just trying to hold you to your New Year's resolution," Danielle teases her.

We finish our breakfast of champions and walk around the corner to our favorite boutique, the Pink Zone. I always gravitate to the part of the store that has plain T-shirts and tank tops, basics in soft cotton that serve my everyday needs.

Today, I migrate over to a rack with dressier items, things I wouldn't normally wear. I pick up a black sleeveless blouse with a deep V-neck and near-sheer fabric. Dare I? Somewhere in the back of my head, a voice cautions me, *You haven't even heard from him in two days.* I choose to ignore that voice and instead make myself concentrate on the doorstep kissing that made me weak in the knees.

I picture wearing the black top with jeans and wedges

and wonder if I can pull it off. It's worth a try; after all, it's on sale, and I still have Christmas money burning a hole in my pocket.

Sloan finds me at the counter. She does a double-take when she sees my purchase.

"Someone's got some explaining to do." Sloan picks up the blouse and calls across the store, "Hey, Danielle, check out what our girl is buying. Looks like we missed a memo."

Danielle comes running over to us. She takes a look at the shirt, then gives me a long look up and down, taking in my sweats, flip-flops, and messy ponytail.

"What's up?" Danielle asks.

"Nothing," I answer. But I let out a little giggle that definitely gives away that something is indeed up.

"Does this have anything to do with Luke Hallstrom?" Sloan homes right in on it.

"Maybe," I say, almost laughing.

I buy the shirt and the girls pull me outside onto a bench.

"Start from the beginning," instructs Danielle.

"And don't leave anything out," adds Sloan.

I am ready to share, so I tell them everything. Every moment, the feel of his lips and of his hands in my hair. Talking about it makes it feel real. And I really want this to be real. Both Danielle and Sloan are listening like it's the best story they've ever heard.

"Wait, how long was the first kiss?" Danielle interrupts.

"I don't know, like maybe two full minutes."

"Did he shove his whole tongue in your mouth?" Sloan asks. "Or did he lightly tease you with it, pulling it in and out?" Sloan always wants the details.

"All I know is that I was melting the entire time."

"I'm melting just listening to this," Danielle says.

"I can't freakin' believe we're talking about Luke freakin' Hallstrom!" Sloan screams.

The screaming and squealing continue on the street corner for the next hour and a half, before Danielle gets serious.

"Are you going to have sex with him?"

"What the heck, Danielle? I don't even know if he likes me. He's probably dating three other girls at the same time."

"He's not," Sloan says. "He and Amanda ended things before college. She took someone else to her sorority formal. He hooked up with Lily Patterson after homecoming, but I think he went home alone after Miles's birthday party."

"How do you know all this?" I ask, incredulous.

"I know things," Sloan says with a shrug.

"Nevertheless, I think it's a little soon to talk about having sex with him. I don't want this to be a hookup. I think I really like him," I say.

"It's never too soon to talk about it. The first time you have sex needs to be planned. You need to be prepared, both mentally and physically, you know what I mean?" Danielle says.

"Danielle, she's not an idiot," Sloan says.

"I know she's not an idiot, Sloan, but there are things she might not think of. Things I didn't think of my first time that would have been helpful."

"Like what?" I ask.

"Well," Danielle starts, "this isn't a hookup. You really like him, so you should take it super slow, make sure he's into you and not just the sex."

Sloan, who was leaning into the conversation, sits back as though to take herself out of it. Sloan knows a lot about hookups, but Danielle has experience with being in a serious relationship.

"You need to know it's coming. Don't let him surprise you or talk you into doing it before you're ready. In fact, the first two or three times he tries, you should say no. He'll respect you for that. When you're ready you should come with protection so he knows you're cool with it. That will turn him on."

Danielle goes on and on, the ultimate expert on a committed, sexual relationship. Throughout the conversation, Sloan continues to retreat. She can't offer much advice on sex, boyfriends, and taking things slowly.

I ask a bunch of laughable questions about logistics, logistics I assume Sloan probably knows just as well as Danielle.

"How will I know when I'm ready?"

"Are we supposed to talk about being exclusive?"

"How do I give a hand job?"

"Do I take my own clothes off, or does he undress me?"

The beautiful thing about having such good friends and feeling so comfortable with them is that I don't have to worry if I sound stupid or naive; I can just get the answers I need.

"Have you guys been texting since you saw him Friday night?" Danielle wants to know.

"No," I say.

"There's been no contact?" Sloan asks, seemingly surprised.

"No, nothing," I say. Now I'm getting even more paranoid. Does that mean something? "I was at the debate all day yesterday, and then came home and crashed."

"You'll probably hear from him today, but don't text him. Let him come to you," Sloan chimes in, but she's a little quieter now, more low-key. Ever since Danielle's lesson on how to be in a relationship, something in Sloan has changed. The sparkly enthusiasm she shared earlier is gone. She doesn't seem excited for me. Am I supposed to feel guilty or apologetic about this thing with Luke, whatever it is? Does this fall in the category of sisters before misters? I wish I could ask Sloan these questions.

CHAPTER THIRTEEN

*L*UKE LOOKS ESPECIALLY CUTE* at track today. I mean, he always looks cute, but today he's wearing a red Nike Dri-FIT shirt that sort of hugs his body, and he's still holding on to that tan from Mexico. Maybe I'm just so into him that he keeps getting better- and better-looking. Or maybe I just didn't look closely enough before.

He's the only one in the high jump area when I finish my last set of hurdles. It's getting dark out, and most people are finished and have either left or are making their way from the track to the locker rooms.

I'm not sure if I should approach him or not. I start stretching as a means of stalling. A long series of calf and quad stretches, followed by a full sequence of back stretches. Still no eye contact from Luke. He seems entirely focused on his high jumps. I'm beginning to think that whatever happened between us is now officially over. I slowly start the dreaded walk back to the locker room. One step. Two. Two and a half. Three.

"Peachy Keen, where're you off to?"

Music to my ears. My heart jumps. I turn around, feigning curiosity, as if to see who in the world might be calling me Peachy Keen.

"I'm finished. Headed home," I say.

"Come over here," Luke says.

I make every effort to walk, not run, in his direction. Coach Chow and the rest of the team are leaving the field as I head over to the high jump mat. We are the only two left.

"I missed you," he says.

What is the right response? I just stand here, looking at him, smiling like a dork.

"What, you've got nothing to say to me?" he teases. "You didn't miss me, too? You don't want to tell me how happy you were that today was Monday so you could come to school and see me?"

Now I continue with the silence, not because I can't think of a witty response (although, truthfully, I can't), but because I'm interested in what else he's going to say. I keep staring at him, wanting to hear more.

"What is this, the silent treatment?" He walks over, scoops me up, and plops me down on the mat. I didn't see that coming. I start to laugh. He lies down next to me, almost over me, and stares into my eyes, his face inches away. I do a quick look around to make sure that we are absolutely alone on the field.

"Sorry we haven't talked. My brother was in town this weekend."

"That's okay," I say, relief calming my every paranoid nerve.

"Did you miss me?" he asks, looking at me with that winning smile.

"I did," I say quietly.

"I gotta say, Peachy Keen, I'm not sure I believe you," he says.

"I missed you," I say with conviction.

"How much?" he asks.

"Tons."

"That's more like it," he says and leans closer, putting his lips over mine in the deepest, sexiest kiss that ever happened. He continues to kiss me, his tongue exploring my whole mouth. He pulls away slightly and delicately licks my lips.

"Mmm, you taste good."

"So do you," I say.

He rolls on top of me, pressing his body against mine, our lips still locked together, our tongues still intertwined. He tastes like a combination of mint and cherry. I love the feeling of his chest against mine. I reach up and put my hands on his back. He's a little sweaty, which I find surprisingly sexy. My natural instincts take over and I lift up his shirt and feel the warm, smooth skin on his back.

"You have soft hands," he says between kisses. He positions his hands under my body and flips me over so that now he's lying on his back and I'm on top of him. His hands start exploring my back, under my shirt, over my jog bra. He skillfully lifts my shirt over my head, removing it completely. I gasp. He looks at me.

"Is this okay?" he asks.

"Yeah," I say.

"You sure?"

"Yeah, I'm sure." I've never been more certain of anything.

He wraps his hands around me, pulling me into him. It's as though I'm fully enveloped in him. The entire world consists of Luke and me and this blue squishy mat. His hands on my body don't feel scary or threatening or uninvited. They feel warm, protective, comforting, and supremely sensual.

"You're a really good kisser," I try to say without breaking my lips away from his. The words end up muddled and muted.

"What was that?" he asks as he pulls away. I can't help but think he's trying not to laugh at me for attempting to kiss and talk at the same time.

"You're a really good kisser," I say, hoping he can't see how awkward I feel.

"It's because I'm kissing you."

He grabs me even tighter and rolls us over again so that he's lying on me, his legs between mine. I open my eyes for an instant and see the stars emerging in the darkening evening sky. I feel his whole body pushing against me. I can tell how much he wants me. I wonder if I should pull back, call it a night, but it's almost impossible to stop something that feels so good.

A faint and familiar clicking noise can be heard in the distance. I don't pay much attention, because right now there's only one thing on my mind, and that thing is on top of me, kissing me passionately and pressing his hips into me. The clicking seems to be getting closer, harder to ignore. Before I realize where the sound is coming from, Luke and I are being sprayed with freezing-cold water.

"The sprinklers!" I yell.

"Who cares?" Luke asks, apparently perfectly happy to stay right where he is.

"You're crazy," I say, laughing, gently pushing him off me. I run across the field through the storm of spraying water. He grabs my shirt and runs after me.

Fifteen minutes later, I walk into my house and my mom calls from the kitchen.

"Janey?"

"Yes."

"Come in here," she says.

I walk into the kitchen and drop my backpack and track bag. Mom is standing over the stove, stirring something in a big pot. Probably pasta. She looks up at me.

"Hi," I say.

"What happened to you?"

I suddenly remember my sopping-wet ponytail.

"I stayed late at the track and the sprinklers went on."

"You stayed late and didn't tell me where you were." She's giving me the firm mom voice. "Have you looked at your phone? I've texted and called you. I was worried."

"Sorry," I say sheepishly.

"Are you?"

"What do you mean?" I ask.

"I mean, you walk in late and wet. It's dark. I tried to reach you and you don't seem to be thinking about anybody but yourself."

"Wow, Mom, that's pretty harsh. I was a little late one night. Give me a break. I made a mistake. I should have checked my phone. I should have let you know. I was at school and then I came home. That's it. It won't happen again."

"Were you with Luke?" she asks pointedly.

"I was."

"I hope that having a boyfriend isn't causing you to make bad choices." It's like she's already making Luke into a villain—as though he's going to pull me to the dark side.

"First, Mom, he's not my boyfriend. Second, I lost track of time. I hardly call that a bad choice."

"Just make sure you're responsible and smart. Like you always have been."

"What's with the overreaction?" I ask.

Mom takes a breath and gives the big wooden spoon another turn.

"I don't know. I guess I'm not used to the fact that you and I live here alone. It feels strange, and a little scary."

"Makes sense. I get it. I'll be more considerate. Anything else?" I ask.

Mom walks closer to me. She twirls my wet ponytail.

"I'm going out Thursday night."

Does my mother have a date? For some reason it's much easier to digest the notion of my dad going on a date. I just can't imagine my mom out with a man other than my dad. She must see the uneasy look on my face.

"I'm just going to dinner with Suzanne and Dana," she says quickly, as though she can read my mind.

I feel myself breathe a huge sigh of relief.

"Then why do you seem so freaked out about it?" I ask.

"I don't know. Every other time I've gone out with the girls, Dad was home with you."

"Mom, that's so untrue. This may be the first time you've gone out since the separation, but there were plenty of times you had dinner with friends while Dad was on trips. I'm seventeen. I can handle an evening at home alone. I have two quizzes and a chemistry lab due Friday. I'll be studying. It's fine. You need to relax."

"You're right. I want to make sure I'm doing this right. That we're communicating and watching out for each other."

"We're fine, Mom. Don't worry so much."

CHAPTER FOURTEEN

BRETT AND I WALK OUT of debate class and down the school hallway. We just mock debated another team in our class, and we kicked their butts. I was definitely in the zone, and it helped that I stayed up until midnight preparing my arguments. We continue walking through the throng of people moving from one class to another as we rehash our coach's comments.

"We need to strengthen our closing—" I barely get the words out before someone grabs me by the hand and pulls me into the empty art room.

Next thing I know, Luke has me up against the Smart Board. I drop my binder on the floor and wrap my arms around his neck. He kisses me hard and fast, as if he wants to get as much in as he can before we both have to get to our next class.

"You smell good," he whispers into my ear. I feel his hands in my hair and his warm breath working its way down my neck, sending goose bumps up my spine.

I press my lips against his, pushing my tongue into his mouth. He opens his eyes wide, surprised by my assertiveness. I am even surprising myself. It feels so good to have his warm, strong body against me. I can't get enough of him.

The doorknob turns and we quickly pull away from each other. I attempt to fix my hair while he grabs my binder off the floor and hands it to me. Art students are filing in for class. No one I really know, but of course several people say hi to Luke.

Before we exit, Luke grabs an oil pastel. He stops me and draws a bright red smiley face on the inside of my forearm.

"See you later, Peachy Keen," he says, and then he walks out the door, leaving me standing there with a goofy grin and messy hair. As soon as I start down the hallway, barely recovering from the most romantic moment (who am I kidding—the only romantic moment) I have ever experienced in the academic building in my school, Brett gets in my face.

"What the hell?" he demands.

"What's the matter?" I ask lamely. If I weren't so rattled, I would have certainly come up with a better, more thoughtful response. At least something that makes sense.

"What's the matter?" he asks. "Hmm. Let's see. You've been distracted and a lot busier than usual the last week or so. I have asked you repeatedly what's going on, giving you several chances to come clean. You have lied to my face over and over, telling me nothing is up other than the crap with your parents. You completely flubbed our debate and I let it go because I felt bad for you. But the truth is you used your parents' separation as a pathetic excuse. And the whole time you were—"

"Brett, I'm sorry," I interrupt.

"It's too late, Janey. I thought we were friends. You don't even tell me you're hooking up with someone. And it's Luke Hallstrom, of all people. That's bullshit."

"It wasn't my intention to keep it a secret from you. I don't know why I didn't say anything. I think I was worried that you'd be . . . I don't know . . . mad or something."

"Mad? Like maybe jealous?"

"No. I don't know." Everything I think to say sounds inane and accusatory. He looks at me with eyes full of disappointment. "I guess I was worried you wouldn't be happy about it," I say lamely.

"I'm not jealous. You're not my type."

"I know. I didn't think you liked me that way, I just—"

"Maybe you didn't tell me because you're embarrassed that you're wasting your time with a worthless, arrogant guy who's going to treat you like shit." He storms off down the hall. I am paralyzed. My feet feel bolted to the floor. The hallway empties out as students find their way to class. I can't move. Why does adding Luke to my life make me feel like I'm losing other people who matter? Is it some kind of sign that this thing with Luke isn't good for me? Maybe I'm not ready for all of this. Maybe I can't handle it. I look down at the bright red happy face on my arm. I wish I felt happy.

That afternoon at track workout, I run hurdles. I see Luke in my peripheral vision, but I force myself to remain focused. I will not let his presence slow me down or distract me. Coach Chow is timing me, and I feel determined not to let Luke cost me seconds on my time. I sense my teammates close behind me, but I will not come in second.

I finish strong and walk over to Coach Chow to get my time. Luke stands with some guys at the Gatorade bins. I'm dying of thirst, but I don't want to walk up to a group of senior boys. I plop myself down on the track and stretch out my calves. Chow is calling out times as other girls finish their hurdles and wind sprints. A shadow is cast over me; someone is shielding me from the hazy late-afternoon sun. I look up, and Luke is standing there with a cup of water.

"Thirsty?" Since the episode in the hallway with Brett, I have felt conflicted, but when I look up and see this gorgeous boy standing here, holding a cup of water, his hair adorably messy and his teeth gleaming white, I go weak. How can he be bad for me?

"Dying." He hands me the water and I gulp it down. "Thanks."

"Nice tat," he says, gesturing at the slightly faded red drawing on my arm.

I look down at the smiley face. "Yeah, it's how girls from my 'hood roll."

He reaches for my hand and pulls me up so I'm standing right in front of him, practically nose to nose, chest to chest. "Let's hang out."

"I can't. My mom is going out tonight and I told her I'd be home to see her before she leaves."

"Wait a second. Your mom's going out?"

"Yes," I say.

"So you'll be home alone?" he asks.

I see where he's going with this. Any fool would.

"Yes again," I say, barely able to meet his eyes.

"Want some company?"

Thoughts of a chemistry lab, a math quiz, and an English quiz race through my mind.

"Yes again."

CHAPTER FIFTEEN

MY MOM IS ACTING SO WEIRD about going out tonight. It's not like I've never been home alone before. She and Dad used to go out to dinner, sometimes just the two of them, sometimes with friends. I think she feels guilty, like she's supposed to be available twenty-four/seven because of the separation. I try to ease her mind without revealing my urgency to rush her out the door. Am I supposed to tell her that Luke is coming over? Ask for permission? I know if I tell her, she'll ask all kinds of annoying questions, circling the subject of safe sex. I am absolutely not ready to have that conversation. There is also the chance that she'll just flat out say that I'm not allowed to be alone in my house with a guy. What do I do in that scenario? Call Luke and say, *Sorry, my mommy won't let me play alone in the sandbox with a boy?* I figure the best plan at this juncture is to keep it quiet.

"I'll be at Ocean View Bar and Grill in Del Mar if you need anything."

"Mom, it's fine."

"I made you a Caesar salad and some chicken skewers."

"Okay, Mom." I want her to hurry up and leave so Luke can come over. The rush of both excitement and fear is flooding my body. I'm going to be alone with a boy in my house. I am terrified. And I can't wait.

Mom kisses me twice on the forehead.

"Love you," Mom says.

"Love you back. Have fun. And don't worry."

"I'll be home by ten. At the very latest."

"Mom. Chill."

And she's gone. I go back to my room and grab my phone to let Luke know my mom is gone. I'm not sure how to word it. *She's gone? Coast is clear?* That sounds so sneaky. *Come on over?* Too desperate. As I struggle with what to say, my phone lights up.

I'm five minutes away. Okay to come over?

All good. My heart is pounding. Am I ready? Do I look okay? I showered and washed my hair when I got home from track practice. I chose my clothes carefully—it didn't make sense to get dressed up only to stay home, but I didn't want to look frumpy in my sweats, so I put on a pair of skinny jeans and a pink Cabo San Lucas tank top. Now that he's almost here, I'm second-guessing myself. Maybe I should make more of an effort to look pretty or, dare I say it, sexy. Maybe I should have blown my hair dry. Too late now. I pull my wet hair into a knot on the top of my head and drag light pink gloss across my lips. Doorbell. Here we go.

Even though I know very well who is at my door, I look out the front window, as I have been trained to do since I was little. Luke, fresh and clean in jeans and a hoodie, is standing on my doorstep holding a pizza box like the cutest delivery boy in the whole world. I open the door.

"I hope you like pepperoni," he says.

"My favorite," I say.

"How'd I guess?"

"Come on in," I say.

We sit at the kitchen table, eating pizza and talking about movies. Luke has seen all the classic movies from the seventies and eighties. He makes me promise that we'll watch *The Godfather* together, a promise I'm more than happy to make. It's surreal to be sitting here eating pizza with Luke Hallstrom at the white Formica table where I've had my breakfast nearly every morning since I was six years old. My nerves have settled and now I'm just happy and comfortable sitting across from him, staring into his beautiful brown eyes.

"Will you show me your room?"

I spoke too soon. My pounding heart is up to its old tricks.

"Sure."

We walk down the hallway to my room. I turn on the light and look at my room as though I'm seeing it for the first time. I see my fluffy white bed piled with pillows and the few stuffed animals I can't part with—the gorilla my dad and I won throwing quarters into jars at the Del Mar Fair and the bear holding a heart reading HUG ME that Danielle bought me for Valentine's Day last year. Neither of us had boyfriends, so we were each other's Valentines. Above my desk hangs a giant corkboard loaded with photos of friends, ribbons from track meets, certificates from debates, ticket stubs, and birthday cards from years past. My running shoes sit in the corner of my room next to a pile of books I've already read but don't want to give away.

I wonder if my room should be somehow more sophisticated. Instead of a bulletin board with souvenirs, perhaps I should have an interesting piece of art hanging above my desk. Or maybe my furniture should look more adult.

"Your room is so you," he says, as though he's delivering the highest of compliments.

"It is?"

"Yeah," he says. "I like it." He sits on the edge of my bed.

"Different from all the other girls' bedrooms?" I say teasingly as I walk over to him.

"Very funny," he says, wrapping his hands around my waist. I'm pretty impressed at how artfully he dodges the subject of his experiences in other girls' rooms. Every time I'm with Luke, either kissing him or looking at his flawlessness, I can't help but wonder what he wants with me. In moments like this, when I am reminded that he's far more experienced than I am, I feel my insecurities rise to the surface. Maybe he has spent a lot of time tangled in the frilly sheets of other girls' beds. That kills me a little. It's great that he's experienced, but I hate feeling like I'm being compared to others—the way I kiss, the way I look, how far I'm willing to go. When I let myself take a turn to negative town, I worry that I'm solely a virgin to conquer.

"I think you're great," he says.

"You do?" I ask with genuine disbelief.

"Yes," he says. "Why is that so hard for you to believe?" he asks.

"I don't know," I say. "I guess I just never thought Luke Hallstrom would be here in my bedroom saying that to someone like me."

"What do you mean, *someone like you?*"

"You know," I say.

"I don't," he says.

"I don't run in the same circles as you. I don't go to parties and hook up with random guys. That time we kissed in the car was the first time I've ever really been kissed."

"Oh, *that's* what you meant," he says with mock realization, as though he's having a major *aha* moment. "I thought you meant someone smart and interesting and totally hot."

I can't help but laugh.

He takes my hand and has me sit down beside him. "Can I kiss you?"

"I was hoping you would."

First he kisses my cheek, then my nose, and then he plants a soft kiss on my forehead. I close my eyes and enjoy the mystery of wondering where the next kiss will land. There it is. Right on my lips. He opens his lips and his tongue finds its way into my mouth. As we sit there kissing I practically inhale him, enjoying the smells of soap and fabric softener. He lies back and gently pulls me so that I'm lying on top of him, his hands in my hair. As we continue kissing, our tongues twisted together, I reach over and switch off the little yellow lamp on my nightstand.

My room goes dark except for the stream of dim light filtering down the hallway from the living room. Luke's hands leave my hair and move to my back. Slowly, slowly they travel from the tops of my shoulders, rubbing my back lightly, softly, sweetly. His strong hands reach the bottom of my tank top, which has ridden up a bit, so I can feel his bare hands on the inch of skin above my jeans. Just the touch of his fingers on the small of my back is enough to make my heart race even faster. And it was beating pretty damn fast already.

His fingers find their way under my tank top and are now working their way back up, only this time directly on my skin. They wander up my back until he has a gentle but firm grasp of my shoulders. In one impressively swift move, he lifts my tank top up and over my head and, before I know it, I am lying on him wearing only jeans and my black no-nonsense bra.

"This okay?" he whispers between deep, soulful kisses.

"Yeah." I manage to eke out the syllable even though practically no sound escapes my lips.

"Here, we'll make it even," he says.

He sits up slightly, gently moving me from lying on top of him to kneeling between his legs. He takes his sweatshirt off, letting it fall to the floor next to my bed. In the dim light, I can barely make out the silhouette of his body, broad and strong and smooth, lying against my pillows. I feel extremely awkward sitting in front of him without my shirt on, even though the room is practically dark. I self-consciously cover my chest, arms crossed, each hand on the opposite shoulder. Luke laughs a little, taking my hands in his, opening my arms wide. Hopefully, in the low light, he can't make out that I'm fully freaked. I'm not scared, and I don't feel forced or pressured. I'm freaked in an excited way. Like I'm on a tropical island, about to jump off a rocky cliff into the crystal-blue water down below. Exhilarated, but unsure whether I'm really ready to take the leap.

"What's the problem?" Luke asks.

"No problem," I say, but I know he's not buying it.

"You don't want me to see your body?"

"I don't think of my body as something that you would want to see," I say.

"Are you kidding me?" he asks in disbelief. He reaches over to the nightstand and turns on my lamp. My hands jump back onto my shoulders like they are on springs.

"Come here," he says. He gets up and guides me over to the mirror that covers the length of the door to my bathroom. He places me in front of the door and stands behind me, his hands interlocked near my bellybutton. "Look at you."

Is he serious? I'm supposed to stand here, wearing jeans and a bra in a fully lit room, and gaze into the mirror at myself with Luke Hallstrom supervising? I don't freakin' think so. I put my hands over my eyes and hope he'll give up on this mission. He takes hold of my hands and pulls them down to uncover my eyes. My lids stay shut tight. I only wish I could make it dark for him as well.

"Will you please open your eyes so you can see what I see?" he begs.

I open my eyes, but look everywhere except at my own reflection—the sandy-beige carpet, the molding around the doorframe, the backward photos reflected in the mirror.

"Come on, just for a second. For me." I finally relent and stare straight ahead.

I try to see in myself what he clearly sees. I look at my image and the self-consciousness slowly evaporates. A blanket of reassurance covers me in warmth and comfort. Everything in the room seems to change, and Luke can obviously pick up on my new sense of ease. He reaches his hands behind my back and unhooks my bra. I keep my eyes locked on the mirror as my bra falls to the floor.

"My god, Janey, look at you." I do as he says and look,

searching to find the truth in his words. It takes significant effort for me to let him stare at me. His hands wrap back around my waist and find their way up to my chest, cupping my breasts. I watch his hands, and then I watch his face. I see how taken he is with me. I see appreciation and admiration in his eyes. Finally his eyes find mine in the mirror. He looks deeply into me, making sure we're in sync. I turn around to face him and feel the whole of my naked chest up against his smooth brown skin. I lift my face to look at him and he delicately licks the tiny space between my lips.

"You're perfect, you know that?" he asks.

"Maybe I'm just perfect for you."

One of the hardest things I've ever had to do was let Luke leave. But it is, after all, a school night, and my chemistry lab is not going to write itself. It's amazing how much energy a topless make-out session can provide. I am burning through my homework when I hear Mom's key in the door.

"Hi," she calls when she steps into the house.

"Hi," I say from my room.

A minute or so passes.

"Where'd the pizza come from?" Uh-oh! I never went back into the kitchen, and the pizza box is still sitting on the counter. No reason to lie, I guess.

"Luke brought it over," I call from my room.

Silence. Footsteps. Mom's face in my doorway.

"Excuse me?" she asks with curiosity more than accusation.

"Luke brought it over. That's fine, isn't it?" I say as though his visit was no big deal.

"Um. Yeah. I guess. It's just a little strange that the first time you have him over is when I'm not home. Seems to me we should have discussed it."

I try to be as casual as possible, like the thought never occurred to me. "Okay. I'll ask you next time. It was no big deal. We ate pizza and then he left so I could do homework." I leave out the best part. However, something tells me my mother and I would have differing opinions about which is the best part. Even though I'm not about to give her specifics of the events that actually transpired, it does not feel good or right to lie to my mother.

"Janey, try to remember I'm not stupid," she says with knowing eyes and a slight smile.

"What are you talking about?" I ask, caught off guard. I feel my face grow hot.

"I'm not about to believe that this boy came over and all you did was eat pizza. I understand that you're not going to tell me everything, but don't play me for a fool."

"Mom . . ." I am at a loss for words.

"It's okay, Janey. You're seventeen and you like a boy. Just remember I was seventeen once, and things aren't that different." She doesn't seem mad, but I still feel extremely guilty.

"We kissed—" I start to say.

"Hey," she interrupts. "I'm not looking for details. Just know I'm aware of what teenagers do. Keep that in mind."

How should I have handled that? This is all uncharted territory, and clearly I am not armed with the tools to navigate it. She stands in my doorway during an extended silence.

"How was your night?" I ask, changing the subject. And just like that, she is back to being an apologetic, newly separated mom, looking at me with big sad eyes, searching for signs of how I'm handling the change in our family life. Little does she know that the dissolution of my parents' marriage is giving me much-needed freedom. Freedom to explore the other part of my life that's unfolding. What's the saying? Every cloud has a silver lining? Luke Hallstrom is my silver lining.

That night I get undressed and, before I put on my pajamas, I go back to the mirror. I stand there naked. This time, I'm alone. There's no gorgeous guy by my side making me feel sexy and wanted. No heat or anticipation in the air. It's just my reflection and me. I see the same body I've always found there, but never took the time to appreciate. The same narrow shoulders, small chest, and muscular legs. I remind myself of Luke's words: *Open your eyes so you can see what I see.* I stare into the mirror and search for the person Luke has found. Slowly, she begins to emerge. A strong, pretty girl is surfacing. Could it be she's always been there?

CHAPTER SIXTEEN

*L*UNCH AT SCHOOL hasn't changed much. Danielle, Sloan, and I always seek one another out and find a spot at the outdoor picnic tables. Brett used to sit with us, but he's been distant since our episode in the hallway. I've tried to be friendly when we have debate, and I've sent him a few random texts, but he's holding a grudge. I see him in the distance eating his lunch on the grass with his friends Noah and Oliver.

Charlie often sits with us because god forbid he miss an opportunity to put his hand on Danielle's ass. Meanwhile, Sloan has been running hot and cold lately. Sometimes she enthusiastically gives details about the hot new science teacher and how she's fairly certain he wants her. Other times, particularly when the subject of Luke arises, she gets frosty and goes tightlipped. I figure I'll give her the space to be moody and she'll come around soon.

Lunch today is like any other. We discuss whether it's better to take the ACT or the SAT.

"I'll suck at either," Charlie says.

"I plan to have Janey take mine for me," Sloan jokes.

"Got room for one more?" It's a familiar voice from directly behind me. I turn around to see Luke standing there, holding a giant sandwich and a shiny red apple.

"Sure." Danielle moves over, practically climbing into Charlie's lap, in order to give Luke plenty of room to sit between us. Sloan perks up a bit. I don't think she's ever been this close to Luke, and, having lusted after him for so long, it's probably kind of a thrill for her to be sitting near him.

"What's everyone talking about?" Luke wants to know.

"Junior stuff. SAT or ACT. Any opinion?" Sloan asks.

"I took the ACT," Luke answers.

"Congrats on BC," Charlie says. I worry it might seem weird that Charlie knows where Luke's going to college. Does Luke think I'm sharing the details of his life with all of my friends? Does he know that news like early admission and an athletic scholarship spreads like wildfire through school and Charlie, a wannabe athlete but indisputable klutz, undoubtedly knew this information long before Luke said two words to me?

"Thanks, man," Luke says, putting down his sandwich and placing his arm around my shoulders. I almost spit out my almonds when I feel his touch. My first reaction is to shrug him off in an effort to keep the secret that we've been hanging out. I have to remind myself that everyone sitting at this table knows what's going on. Of course, they don't know that last night Luke took my shirt off and felt my boobs. Although that's hardly relevant right now.

"You're going to run track there?" Charlie asks.

"That's the hope," Luke says.

As the guys continue their conversation, Danielle and I catch each other's eyes and fight the urge to laugh out loud. Sloan gives me an excited, stifled smirk, and I know that she's thinking, *Oh my f-ing god, that guy is so hot and he's so into you.* I appreciate that Sloan is sharing in the excitement, because it would suck if she got jealous and bitchy.

From across the patio, I see Luke's friend Zach Nelson approaching. It looks like he's coming over to us, but I can't be certain. I haven't officially met Zach, but I know he and Luke have been friends since middle school. Zach is on the football team and is hoping to walk on at a Division I school next year. Luke talks about Zach sometimes, how much fun they have together and how much he respects that Zach works really hard on the field because he's not a naturally gifted athlete. As Zach nears, his girlfriend, Emily, also someone I've never met but know all about, catches up to him. Holding hands, they walk over to us.

"What's up?" Zach asks, sitting down on the other side of Sloan. Emily stands behind Zach, hands on his shoulders. I can tell she's as unsure as I am about this random group and why we are gathered around the same lunch table. She notices Luke's arm around me and gives me a long once-over, as though I'm a complete stranger. It's clear she's never seen me before in her life. High school is funny that way. We know names, stats, and details about many of the kids who are older, particularly people like Luke, Zach, and Emily. But we rarely have that information about people younger than we are. Now Emily, who I happen to know is a volleyball player and has had many boyfriends (I know this because there are always a lot of public displays of affection at school), is giving me a *Who the hell are you?* look.

Similarly, Zach assesses the group around the table. Particularly Sloan, Danielle, and me. "So, you guys are all juniors?" he asks.

"Yep," Sloan answers, taking a sip from her water bottle.

"Do you know any cute girls for our friend Miles?"

Luke jumps in. "Zach. Seriously, man?"

"What?" Zach asks innocently. "What's the problem?"

"You want them to pimp their friends out to Miles?" Luke asks.

"I was just curious," Zach says.

"Miles can find his own action," Luke says.

"I may know someone," Sloan says with a grin.

"E.B.," Danielle cautions.

"E.B.?" Luke asks curiously, popping the last bite of his sandwich into his mouth.

"E.B.?" Zach echoes.

"Inside joke," I say.

"Well, that's no fair. Please explain," Luke says, looking at me with that Hallstrom sparkle in his eye.

"No way!" Sloan says quickly, staring at me hard, as though she fears I might give in to Luke's charm.

By the end of lunch, a mere twenty minutes later, before Emily and Zach walk away, Emily turns to me and says, "We should all hang out."

"Yeah, sure," I say.

What does that even mean? Does she want to double date with Luke and me? Is she suggesting everyone from the lunch table, including Sloan, Danielle, and Charlie, hang out together? Have I entered new social strata now that I'm dating Luke? Am I now accepted into this group of senior celebrities? I guess, somewhere in my subconscious brain, I figured my friends and Luke would never intersect, thus I could continue to avoid navigating the choppy waters that result when my worlds collide.

The following Friday night, I find myself in the back seat of Zach Nelson's Toyota FJ Cruiser. Zach and Emily are in the front, and Luke is next to me. Again, I feel too young and awkward to be in this group, but Luke tries to make me feel comfortable. He keeps grabbing my hand and telling me how great I look. Getting dressed was a challenge. Thank god Sloan came over to help. In a way, I was dressing more with Emily in mind than Luke. Emily always looks so sophisticated and glamorous. She always has the right jeans, the right sweater, and the right scarf thrown haphazardly around her neck. Even when she's in her volleyball uniform, she looks like a model.

Sloan had to practically force me to wear the new top I bought in La Jolla. It was so fun to purchase it, but then every time I saw it hanging in my closet it practically mocked me, as if to say, *You know you're never going to have the guts to wear me.* That top—softer, sheerer, and lower-cut than my other clothing—looked like it just didn't belong in my wardrobe. The tags still hung from the neckline, tempting me to return it. But Sloan would not take no for an answer, so I really had no choice. We paired it with dark skinny jeans and Sloan's black suede boots. I have to admit, even though I feel like I am playing dress-up, I like the way I look. I actually feel pretty.

As we near the restaurant, Zach and Emily start arguing in the front seat. Something about the music on the radio.

"Why did you change that song?" Emily whines.

"Because Taylor Swift is weak," Zach says.

"You know I love that song."

"So what? I want to listen to real music."

"But if you know I love it, you should want me to be happy," Emily says with real anger in her voice.

Their argument continues as Zach pulls the car into the parking lot. Am I really listening to this? Are two reasonably sane people really having a legitimate fight about something so ridiculous? It escalates and Zach tells her she's being a bitch. I am so uneasy, not sure what I'm supposed to be saying or doing. Maybe they forgot we were sitting back here.

"We'll meet you in there," Luke says, opening the door and getting out. He holds the door open for me and before he shuts it he says, "By the way, Zach, you're the one being a bitch." We escape from the tension-filled SUV into the comfort of a red leather booth in the crowded Italian restaurant.

"Sorry about that," Luke says as though it's his fault.

"That was crazy," I say.

"They fight like that all the time."

"What's the point? Why be with someone who makes you so unhappy?" I ask.

"Guess they like making up," he says, and a sly smile indicates just the kind of making up he is imagining.

"Very funny. Have you ever been in a relationship where you fought like that?" I ask him.

"I've only had one other real relationship, and no, not much drama."

He must be talking about Amanda McKay. They were always together last year. She was a senior and he was a junior. I would see them holding hands walking down the hallway, and sometimes kissing at her locker. She was always the lead in the school musicals. I went to see *Grease* last year, and I remember seeing him waiting for her after the show with a huge bouquet of flowers.

"That's a good thing," I say.

"Yeah, it was mostly good. She was older. Taught me a lot. She was my first real relationship. And my first, well, everything."

I immediately feel a surge of self-doubt. She was his first. You always remember your first. Tough to compete with that.

"Where is she now?"

"Right around the corner, at UCSD." Ugh! It gets worse!

"Do you still talk to her?"

"Yeah, sometimes. She's busy. I'm busy. But we check in, stay in touch. She's a great girl. Super talented."

I'm noticing that Luke doesn't have a bad thing to say about anyone. He's everyone's best friend, and most likely the subject of many girls' fantasies. I'm beginning to think being the guy who girls want to be with and other guys want to be like is a top priority for him. I see him flashing his million-dollar smile at girls in school. He always throws an arm around someone in an affectionate act of friendship that is no doubt the highlight of the day for the lucky owner of that shoulder.

"Why did you break up?"

"She went away for the summer, so we weren't even going to see each other, and then she was starting college. It just sort of made sense to give each other freedom, and then it turned into a friendship. Very gradual. No big teary breakup."

I think about Luke graduating high school, going to the East Coast for the summer, and then starting college. I guess it will make sense for us to break up, too. The thought is too awful to even consider.

"Was that your only girlfriend?"

"Well, that was my only serious relationship," he says with a smirk.

"So that means there have been some comedic ones?" I ask, trying to be light even though I'm grilling him about his romantic past.

"Ha, ha. It only means there were people I hung out with, but it never got serious."

"Care to give me a name?" I ask.

"Do I have to?" he asks, smiling. He probably knows there's really no upside to having this conversation.

"No," I say, and I mean it. It's not my intention to barrage him with questions. I'm just incredibly curious about his colorful past when mine is so monochromatic.

"Julia."

"Julia Zimmer, as in student body president?" I ask in disbelief.

"That's the one."

"You mean to tell me that Julia allows something in her life to be *not* serious?"

"Trust me, Julia Zimmer is not looking to be tied down," he says.

My mind races. I assume that means that Luke and Julia

were (are?) having casual sex. So Luke has had sex with at least two people. Amanda McKay, the Meryl Streep of La Jolla High, and Julia Zimmer, leader of the teenage free world. Who knows? Maybe more. For those of you keeping score at home, that's Luke: 2+, Janey: 0.

CHAPTER SEVENTEEN

THE BEST PART OF MY DAY at school is when Luke sees me from across the courtyard and gives me a flirtatious glance. Or when he passes me in the hall and squeezes my arm without anyone else noticing. But as much as I love the constant reminders that he's into me, there is a worrisome paranoia that Brett might be nearby, witnessing and judging. I want to make things right with Brett. I am not willing to throw twelve years of friendship away without a fight. I feel like I have to make the effort, show Brett that I'm willing to go to battle to get my friend back.

Brett and I have always watched horror movies together, both at home and in the movie theater. My other friends are just not interested in screaming their heads off in fear, so Brett is my go-to scary-movie buddy. Whenever one of us is home flipping through channels and comes across *Insidious, The Ring,* or *Paranormal Activity,* we fire off a text to the other and, together, relish a moment or two of terror.

One Wednesday night after dinner, I delay my math homework and the crucial need for a shower and go to the living room to channel surf. *The Exorcist* has just started. This is the perfect opportunity to reach out to Brett. He and I watched *The Exorcist* together when we were ten. Big mistake. We were at his house and his parents were having a New Year's Eve party. We were bored hanging out with the grownups, so we went to the playroom to watch television. We found *The Exorcist* and, full of false courage, thought it was an excellent and very daring choice.

We later realized that both of us were too embarrassed to admit that we were completely freaked out, so we powered through the whole movie, each of us suffering in silence. I called my dad to pick me up as soon as the movie ended, and I went home trembling. I slept in my parents' bed for the next two weeks, never confessing the cause of my sudden anxiety. I was afraid I would get Brett in trouble if I told my parents that we had watched *The Exorcist*.

The fact that this, of all movies, is on right now is definitely a sign that it's time to make up with Brett. I take out my phone and make a video of the scene where Regan pees on the floor. I text the video to Brett. No other words, emoji, or comments, just nineteen seconds of the movie. I clutch my phone, waiting for him to reply. Within seconds I see the telltale three dots indicating that he is typing. I am fraught with nerves, anticipating his response. Finally it comes: *Pause it—I'm on my way.*

In ten minutes, Brett and I are sitting on my sofa watching Linda Blair's character bounce around on her bed, screaming obscenities at priests. Are we supposed to discuss our fight? Is he expecting me to say I'm sorry? I don't think either of us owes or deserves an apology. I just think we have to accept each other as things change in our lives.

When the movie ends, and Brett and I are adequately freaked out, I turn off the television and turn to him.

"Thanks for coming over," I say.

"I could never let you watch that movie alone," he says. "I'm permanently scarred from the first time we saw it."

"Me too."

There's a long pause, but not an awkward or uncomfortable one. It feels like we're both happy to be occupying the same space for the first time in a long time.

"So," he says, "Luke Hallstrom."

"Yeah," I say.

"Pretty crazy." He leans back on the sofa and puts his feet up on the coffee table.

"I know," I agree. He's right. It is a little crazy.

"What's *that* like?" He keeps the tone light, but it's obvious to me that he's not so much curious as he is critical.

"It's good," I say.

"Really?" he asks in disbelief.

"Yeah, he's really sweet."

"Well, yeah," he says, like I've just mastered the obvious.

"What does that mean?" I ask him, knowing I'm not going to like his answer.

"I mean of course he's sweet. You're a girl and he wants to sleep with you." I pick up a pillow and hit him on the head. "Am I wrong?" he asks.

"We aren't there yet," I say.

"Good."

"Why *good?*" I want to know.

"Because you're a nice girl and I don't want him corrupting you," Brett says.

"What are you, my father?" I give him another smack with the pillow. He pulls the pillow out of my hand and puts it behind his head.

"I care about you, and I don't want you to be one of those stupid girls who loses a sense of who she is and what she wants as soon as some popular older guy tries to have sex with her."

"I'm not."

"You're not a stupid girl or you're not going to have sex?" Now he's smiling. He's teasing me, which I know means he's no longer mad.

"Either," I say, returning his smile.

"Good to know," he says. "Stay that way." He takes the pillow from behind his head and throws it right in my face.

I've heard parents and teachers refer to the years from puberty to adulthood as the *formative years.* I suppose that means that it's a transitional period that shapes the kind of adults we turn out to be. If that's the case, then we all need to give one another a break. We're going to change and grow and make mistakes. We're going to start and end relationships. We're going to reinvent ourselves. Real friends need to give each other room to screw up, blossom, change, and figure out who we want to be.

CHAPTER EIGHTEEN

SUNDAY-NIGHT DINNER WITH DAD. Now that a few weeks have passed since Dad moved out, I guess he's feeling less apologetic about the separation and eventual divorce, because he rejects my plea for sushi. When we got back from Cabo, my parents were walking on eggshells around me, bending over backward to make sure I was content and my every wish was their command. Even though my house felt empty and sad, there were a few enjoyable side effects. Like my dad's willingness to let me choose the restaurant.

Tonight we go to a super-casual Korean barbecue place that we've been to about a million times before. Dad's idea is to get the food to go and take it back to his new apartment. I'm not at all excited to see his new place. I picture a total woman trap with speakers in every room and a bearskin rug in front of a roaring fire. Not that my dad is that type at all. I've never even seen him notice an attractive woman. I remember years ago when I was at the beach with my mom and dad, and a girl walked by in a tiny white see-through bikini, with a bronze fake tan and massive boobs swaying from side to side. My mom and I exchanged a glance and a giggle. My dad, however, never even looked up from the latest issue of *The New Yorker*. He used to stare at my mom as though he was constantly caught off guard by her beauty, but never seemed to notice a hot piece of ass nearby.

With our piping-hot Korean takeout in hand, we pull into the underground parking garage in his building and ride the elevator up to the third floor. His apartment is airy and sparkling clean. Everything looks and smells new. There is a beautiful view of the La Jolla Cliffs and the Pacific Ocean. It's so strange to have to remind myself that the furniture, the art on the walls, and the kitchen appliances are his and his alone. These items have no history of being part of a family or a household, unlike all the things that fill the rooms and line the shelves in what is now my house. This place has a very cool beachy feel, with warm earth tones and lots of natural light coming in through the sliding glass doors facing the water.

I sit down on the beige tweedy sofa and put our cardboard containers on the glass coffee table. I am just about to dig in to the food when Dad stops me.

"Don't you want to see your room?"

"Oh. Yeah. Sure," I say.

There are doors on either side of a short hallway. To the left is my dad's room. It's done in brown and tan, with dark wood shutters and a big mahogany dresser topped with several framed photos of me. My room is small and simple; the bed is tucked into the corner and topped with a fluffy cream-colored down comforter and a bunch of little pillows in various shades of pale blue and green. There's an empty corkboard on the floor, propped against the wall.

"Dad, I love it. It's so cool."

"Decorate the room however you like. I want you to be comfortable here."

"Okay, thanks."

"I hope that board will soon be covered in pictures and ribbons and ticket stubs," he says.

I know how important it is to him that I feel at home. I give him a big hug and we head back to the living room to eat our dinner. Even though I would have preferred a spicy tuna roll, the Korean barbecue is really quite tasty.

"I'm sure it's strange to be here, but I hope you'll eventually see this as your place, too."

"It's a little weird," I say, "but it's cool. I like this place." I imagine coming here after school, doing homework out on the balcony with the ocean in the distance. I wonder if Luke will ever be here with me. If he'll ever lie next to me on that bed down the hall.

"So, what's going on in your life?" Dad asks, as if he has a front-row seat to the scandalous thoughts racing through my brain.

"Nothing."

"What about the boy?"

"And what boy are you referring to, exactly?" I ask, fully aware that my mom has probably kept my dad up to speed on all matters Luke.

"The boy who brought the pizza while mom was out." I rest my case.

"Luke," I say.

"Luke. He's the one I met after sushi, right?"

"Right," I say.

"What's going on with him?" Dad asks. I know most teenage girls don't discuss sex and romance with their dads. I certainly have no intention of filling him in about all that, but I've always been able to talk to him about everything. I told him, not my mom, about Tyler Stone and the umbrella.

"I like him," I say with genuine honesty and vulnerability.

"Be careful. Be safe."

"I will, Dad."

"Remember: Just because I don't live with you doesn't mean I'm not available to you whenever you need me. You know that, right?" he says.

"Yes, I know." We laugh as we finish our bowls of spicy noodles and veggies.

"Wanna sleep here tonight? I'll take you to school tomorrow."

"Sure. Sounds good."

CHAPTER NINETEEN

MY DAD DROPS ME OFF in the usual spot and Sloan is waiting, looking perturbed.

"Where were you last night?" she asks with accusation and suspicion.

I am totally in the dark as to why she seems so angry.

"I slept at my dad's." My own words sound foreign to me.

"I texted you like fifty times and you never responded."

"My phone died and I didn't have my charger." I'm not sure why I'm defending myself. "What's the problem?"

"I thought you were with your *boyfriend,*" she says bitterly.

"First, he's not my boyfriend, and second, why would that make you so angry?"

"Because you're changing, Janey. You don't have time for your friends anymore." She is seething with irritation, and I honestly have no idea what I've done wrong.

Now I'm the one getting angry. I wasn't even with

Luke last night. What I can piece together in my brain is that Sloan tried to reach me, and when I didn't respond, she figured I was with Luke and was purposely ignoring her. It's almost like she's looking for a reason to be mad at me.

"Yes, Sloan. I have been spending time with Luke. And, yes, the simple math tells us that, as a result, I have less time for other things. I don't know what we officially are, if anything. Who knows how long it will last, but I do like him, and I would think a true friend would understand that and be happy for me," I say, surprised at my own ability to speak directly and strongly to her.

She looks so angry that her eyeballs might burst from the steam building up in her head. "So your friends are just supposed to take a back seat, be your second choice, or third, or fourth, and sit around and wait for you to grace us with your presence?"

"That's not what I said. I just think friends should be understanding," I say, trying to remain calm.

She gets an icy, resigned look on her face, takes a deep breath, and says through gritted teeth, "I'm not the shitty friend here, Janey. *You* are." She turns and walks ever so slowly into school.

I am frozen. I have a lump in my throat and a sickening feeling in my stomach, as though I swallowed a rock. I don't want to cry. Just as one part of my life starts to flourish, everything else goes down the toilet. First, my mom is clearly worried that her angelic daughter is being corrupted. Then Brett gets pissed at me for being secretive. And now Sloan tells me I'm a shitty friend. Have I really done so much wrong? Am I supposed to walk away from Luke to maintain the status quo and thus make *other* people happy?

I don't even see Danielle and Charlie approach from the parking lot.

"Hey," Danielle says. "You okay?"

Just the sound of her voice makes me burst into tears. Big, fat, sloppy tears. The kind that come with shortness of breath and a runny nose.

"Charlie, I'll meet you at break," Danielle tells him, and he takes the not-so-subtle hint to make a swift exit from the girl drama.

Danielle pulls me into the bathroom and I fill her in on my conversation with Sloan.

"She'll come around. She just needs to get used to it," Danielle assures me.

"Did she do this with you when you started dating Charlie?"

"She was a little bitchy, but your situation might be worse, because she's always had a fantasy about Luke. I promise you, she's not looking to lose your friendship over this."

"She's got a funny way of showing it," I say.

"Maybe she's struggling with the fact that you and I both have someone right now and she doesn't."

"Maybe"—I sniffle—"but is that my fault?"

"Of course not," Danielle soothes.

Danielle stays with me until I get myself together after a marathon cry. We spend the entire first period in the bathroom, and I feel bad making Danielle miss class, but she says she is more than happy to skip studio art. The last time I cried like that was when I was eight years old and I found a puppy on the street and my parents made me give it back to its owners. Luckily, Danielle is the type of girl who not only brings a purse to school, but in that purse, she happens to have all the items that might come in handy after a surprise blubbering session. My nose runs so much when I cry that I've been wiping and blowing it for the last twenty minutes. As a result, the skin under my nostrils is bright red, so Danielle's concealer is a godsend. She expertly dabs at my splotches with her cover-up wand and, presto, good as new. Thanks to Danielle's Visine, my red, watery eyes are now as clear as if I'd just awakened from a twelve-hour slumber.

We wait until we hear the bell ring and the sounds of students filling the halls between classes. We make a quick exit from the bathroom and I walk over to my locker. I see Sloan at her locker, about ten yards away. I give her a look that begs, *Can't we just get along?* She stares right through me for half a second before she turns and starts talking to Brian Burger, the computer genius who happens to have a locker right next to hers. I can't imagine what Sloan and Brian could possibly be talking about, but it looks like he's hanging on her every word.

"Good morning. Did you sleep in or something?" Luke walks up from behind me and takes me by surprise. I have been standing here like a fool watching Sloan and Brian engaged in what seems to be a riveting conversation.

"Oh, hi. No, I just skipped English this morning. Long story." I don't want Luke to know that I had a complete meltdown and that he was actually at the center of the drama.

"You okay?" he asks.

"Yeah," I say a little too quickly, worried that the floodgates might open again.

"What's your next class?" he asks.

"Math."

"Come on, I'll walk you." He interlaces his fingers in mine, and we walk. Holding hands. We are now a teenage couple making our debut on the stage that is the high school hallway. It clearly doesn't faze him that this is a sort of announcement at school. I, on the other hand, am dying inside. I wonder if he has any idea how significant this little stroll is to me.

Part of me feels unbelievably lucky to have Luke making a public statement about how much he likes me. The other part of me is extremely uncomfortable being on display in this way. I don't know where to look.

I see Bella Ruben, who was my next-door neighbor from the time I was in preschool until fourth grade, when her family bought a big house with a swimming pool.

We used to make mud pies in her backyard and lemon-ade stands in the driveway. Bella gives me look as if to say, *Nice going, Janey.*

The most awkward part of our walk down the hallway is passing Sloan. She pretends not to notice, but her eyes go right to my hand in Luke's. She quickly looks away. Other people are less practiced at hiding their surprise. We get our share of smiles, raised eyebrows, and whispers. I notice a few nods from senior girls, like I've been accepted into an exclusive club. It's as though all of a sudden, I matter. I was no one when I was just Janey King. Or when, in the final track meet of the season, I won the three-hundred-meter low hurdles as a freshman. Or when I took the top speaker prize at a debate. But as soon as I've been endorsed by the one and only Luke Hallstrom, I am someone.

It doesn't seem like Luke is at all aware of the state-ment he is making. Luke does what feels right to him, and he's not going to worry about being judged. I love that about him. And I love holding his hand at school, and I love that we have nothing to hide, and I think I might love him.

That afternoon, I walk out of the locker room on my way to the track and Luke is standing there, arms crossed, dressed to work out.

"Hi," I say. "What's up?"

"I don't feel like doing the same old boring workout."

"Okay," I say, wondering where he's going with this. My mind races. I won't let a suggestion from Luke keep me from doing the right thing. "I need to get a run in."

"Me too," he says. "I just can't do high jumps today. I need to mix it up."

"We could run at Torrey Pines," I suggest. There is the most beautiful eight-mile stretch of looping dirt trails along the coast. The narrow path winds over and around the oceanfront cliffs, shaded by huge pine trees.

"Genius. Grab your stuff."

It's a great afternoon for a run by the water. The sun is hanging low in the sky, and there is a cool breeze lifting off the ocean and onto my body, which is getting warmer and sweatier with each mile. I run in front of Luke on the narrow path. There was a time, probably only a few weeks ago, when I would have felt really self-conscious knowing Luke was right behind me. I might have worried what I looked like from behind, how my form was being judged by him. But now I simply enjoy the moment. Gorgeous scenery, Luke at my heels, the smell of the Pacific Ocean wafting through the air. Nothing else matters.

I think about our walk earlier today, the one where we strolled down the hall at school, raising curiosity and interest among our classmates. That walk was merely twenty yards down a fluorescent-lit hallway lined with orange lockers and the cacophony of voices, books dropping, and doors opening and closing. It lasted only three minutes, but seemed to go on forever. Now we are on an entirely different kind of journey. It's just the two of us on eight miles of gorgeous coastline. The only sounds are those of the sea and our footsteps on the soft ground, and I can already tell it's going by much too quickly.

When I see the end of the run in the distance, I kick into high gear and sprint the last quarter mile. The vibrations of Luke's footsteps grow fainter. I run harder, faster, stronger. Unlike in the school hallway, I am completely at ease on this mission. I know where to go, where to look, how fast to travel. I sprint to the tree where Luke and I dropped our water bottles and sweatshirts. I finish and sit down in the shade to catch my breath. I see Luke approaching and lean back on my elbows in a pose that suggests I've been waiting around for him all day. He runs right for me, pretends to crash into the tree, and falls on top of me.

"Ugh, I'm so sweaty," I protest.

"I like your sweat," he says, drawing a finger down my damp arm.

"Are you crazy? I'm so gross."

"There's nothing gross about you," Luke says, and he licks the back of my neck under my ponytail, sending chills up my spine. I hear a moan escape my lips, conveying to him, as well as myself, how good he makes me feel. I close my eyes and let my head fall forward as the sensations travel to my every nerve. He continues to run his tongue around my neck, making his way to my ear and ultimately finding my mouth.

My eyes are still closed when I feel his lips touch mine, and I kiss him hungrily. The feelings he has sent through my skin into my veins have made me ravenous for him. I press my lips firmly against his as my tongue explores every crevice of his mouth.

"Get a room," I hear someone say, and I open my eyes to see two guys, probably in their thirties, running by. Luke and I start laughing, too caught up in our moment to feel embarrassed.

"Should we get out of here?" he asks.

"Yes, please," I say.

When we get back to my house, I notice that my mom's Volvo is not in the driveway. Then I vaguely remember her saying something this morning about parent/teacher conferences after school today. I think she might have said she'd be home around dinnertime. I really need to start paying more attention when she speaks.

"I'm pretty sure we have an hour or so to ourselves," I tell Luke.

"I can think of a few things to do with that time," he says with a twinkle in his eye.

I take Luke to the backyard, where we have a fire pit and a canopied lounge chair big enough for two. He sits down and leans back against the lounge as I hand him one of the water bottles I grabbed from the fridge. I sit down in front of him on the lounge. When we first moved in, my dad planted cypress trees along the perimeter of our backyard, and now the trees are huge and create a living wall that makes the yard totally private.

"It's cool back here," he says.

"Thanks. If you're lucky, I'll make you s'mores one day."

"Hope I get lucky." We both laugh at the choice of words. "You're awesome," he says.

"Thanks," I say. "So are you."

"You think so?" he asks.

"I think everyone does," I say.

"I'm not so sure about that. I bet you could find a few haters out there." Just the way he says it, I can tell he himself doesn't believe it. Again, I'm reminded that Luke is fully invested in being universally adored.

"I doubt that. What's not to like?"

"Well, same goes for you," he says.

"Not exactly," I say, and I mean it.

"Oh, please," he says. "You're so smart, so cute, so down-to-earth."

"What do you mean *down-to-earth*?"

"You're not caught up in all the crap I hear other girls talking about. You know, clothes and purses and their flat-ironed hair. And you have no insecurities."

I am stunned. Does he really believe that? "You're blind! I have so many insecurities."

"Name one."

"Just one?" I ask.

"One."

"Okay, here's one. Today, when you held my hand on the way to math, I worried that people wondered what you were doing with a nobody like me." I surprise myself with my ability to look him straight in the eye and reveal how self-conscious I am.

"First, you shouldn't worry about what other people think. Second, anyone with half a brain knows damn well that I'm the lucky one to have you as my girlfriend."

"Your girlfriend?" I ask.

"I guess I should have thought of a better way to bring that up. I think of us and boyfriend and girlfriend. Don't you?"

"I wasn't sure," I say.

"Well, what do you want us to be?" he asks.

"I'd like to be your girlfriend," I say.

Ever since our earliest moments together, I've worried that Luke would never like me the way I was growing to like him. But in the last instant, all of that changed. He is my boyfriend. I am his girlfriend. This is real. And yet, it still feels like a fantasy.

He lifts my chin so that our faces are less than an inch apart. "Just to be clear, I'm the lucky one," he says in a whisper, and he kisses me softly, lightly, as if to punctuate his point. I kiss him back and the soft kisses grow more intense, more passionate. "Should we take off our sweaty shirts?"

"For sure," I say and I reach for his shirt, pulling it over his head. He then helps me off with my shirt and jog bra, leaving our sticky bodies to cool in the brisk February air. He explores my skin, front and back. I love the feeling of his hands on my back, my chest, and my shoulders. We wrap our arms around each other and the kissing continues, creating more heat between us.

"I have a question," he says.

"What?"

"Are your shorts sweaty too?"

Is my heart beating fast because I'm nervous or excited? Or both? "Yeah, a little," I say.

"Mine too." He lifts his hips and slides his shorts off. He's wearing black boxer briefs that hug his body and make his erection beyond obvious. It's one thing to assume it's there, or to feel a slight hardness pressed against me through his jeans. It's an entirely different matter to see a huge boner underneath a thin layer of black cotton. And that boner is pointed at me. It's a turn-on, but it's also a little scary. "Lean back," he says.

I lean back so my head is at the foot of the lounge. He leans over me and reaches his hands into my shorts, easing them off my body. I'm so glad I happen to have cute underwear on today. It could have easily been the ugly faded pink ones with the lace coming loose at the edge.

Once my shorts have been discarded, Luke lowers himself onto me. His face on my face, his chest on my chest, his hips on my hips. Even with the cool breeze, I feel myself getting hotter and sweatier. He is rubbing against me, pressing himself with a seasoned rhythm. I feel like I'm going to explode. My legs separate slightly and he fits snugly between them. I can feel the warmth beneath our underwear. Is it coming from me or from him? Or is it the fusion of our body parts? I picture us like those commercials for pain relievers where there is a red throbbing epicenter under a crude drawing of a unisex form, and arrows shoot outward depicting the pain spreading through the body. Only in our case, there is this intense heat arising from between our legs and spreading outward from there.

"Should we stop?" he whispers in my ear. Although the pressing and rubbing do not appear to be stopping.

"That's probably a good idea," I say.

We slowly sit up, facing each other, taking a moment while our breathing returns to normal and our inner temperatures cool. Another moment passes while we sit there in our underwear.

"I don't want your mom to come home to this. Not the best way for me to make a first impression."

"Yeah, good point." We gather our clothes from the ground. Getting dressed is not nearly as sexy as getting undressed. I feel so weird stepping into my shorts and slipping on my shirt in front of him. There's really no graceful way put on sweaty clothes.

When we both have our shorts and shirts back on, Luke sits down to put on his shoes. "Come here," he says, tapping the space next to him on the lounge cushion. I sit.

"What?" I say with curiosity.

"I want to talk to you for a second." Oh god. Nothing good has ever started with *I want to talk to you for a second*. Here it comes. He didn't mean it. He doesn't want things to be that serious. He wants to take it back. I feel my stomach tense up like my body is getting itself ready for a punch to the gut.

"What's up?" I ask as casually as possible.

He looks into my eyes; I swear he can see through me. "I want to have sex with you." I almost fall off the lounge. "Let me rephrase that. I want to make love to you. I know how important the first time is, and I want to be your first. I promise to be gentle and patient and wait until you're ready."

"Wow" is all I can think to say. I have gotten an A on practically every vocabulary test, essay, paper, and grammar quiz in my entire life, and all I can muster in this moment is one silly word.

"That's it?" he asks.

"I want to have sex with you, too. I want you to be my first. I trust you, and I want to remember for the rest of my life that my first time was with you, because you make me feel really comfortable. I don't know when I'll be ready, and I hope you'll wait, but I have a feeling it won't be too long."

"It can be as long as you want," he says, and I believe him.

"Okay," I say.

"One more thing," he says.

"Yes?"

"Your shorts are on inside out. You might want to fix that before your mom comes home," he says, smiling.

"Oh god!" I say. I am so embarrassed. I was sitting here having a serious conversation with Luke about sex while wearing my shorts inside out. I look down and see that the mesh built-in underwear is lamely hugging my body while the black nylon hangs out from underneath. Could anything look less sexy? What do I do?

"I'll be right back," I say.

I practically sprint into the house to my bedroom, where I sit on the bed for a minute, positively mortified. Realizing I can't leave Luke outside, I compose myself, take off all my running clothes, and throw on a pair of leggings and a sweatshirt. I do not want to walk back outside, but I know I don't have a choice. I can't just hide from him, hoping he'll forget the humiliating image of me; I know I won't soon forget.

When I leave my bedroom, I see Luke walking from the backyard to the front door.

"Are you leaving?" I ask.

"I didn't know if I'd ever see you again," he jokes.

"That was really embarrassing," I say.

"Don't worry about it," he assures me.

"Easy for you to say," I say. "You were all right-side-in."

"So you're saying you can be practically naked in front

140

of me, but you can't wear your shorts inside out?" he asks, a crooked grin on his lips.

There goes Luke again, finding the right words to say to put me at ease and make the awkward moments funny and fine. At the same time, I know I will never wear those shorts again.

"Ironic, right?" I say.

Now I officially have a boyfriend. Luke Hallstrom is my boyfriend. I am his girlfriend. Something I never thought I wanted or needed is making me so happy. The crazy part is that it doesn't alleviate my insecurity like I thought it would. I always figured girls who had boyfriends didn't have to worry about having a bad hair day or waking up with a pimple, because they knew there was someone who loved them no matter what. What I'm learning is that having a boyfriend makes me worry about that superficial stuff even more. If I say something wrong or wear something ugly or put my shorts on inside out, am I going to lose the thing I never even thought I wanted in the first place?

CHAPTER TWENTY

ON THE WEEKENDS when Danielle doesn't have dance competitions, her Friday afternoons are free, and we hang out after school. Our usual plan is to go the mall, get a beverage or a bite, and walk in and out of the shops. Our usual plan also includes Sloan. I hate that Sloan and I have been avoiding each other. My phone seems so quiet now that it's not lighting up with texts from her with constant updates about where she is, what she's doing, and what she's eating, and funny comments about cute boys, bitchy girls, and annoying parents.

"What's she doing this weekend?" I ask Danielle. She knows exactly who the *she* is in this question without my having to specify.

"I don't know," she says unconvincingly.

"Yes, you do," I press.

"I invited her to come today, but she said she was going to hang out at home to catch up on *America's Next Top Model* reruns."

"Sounds fun," I say dryly. It stings to know she'd rather

watch television reruns than spend time with her supposed best friends.

We grab iced lattes and walk around the mall for a while, dipping into shops and browsing through racks of clothes, shelves of makeup, and displays of shoes. Danielle tells me how she and Charlie can never be together at her house because the twins think it's hilarious to spy on them or rifle through the trash in search of used condoms.

"I swear, I think my parents have given up. It's like they're too exhausted to enforce any discipline. Those boys are totally out of control," she says.

"I know they drive you crazy," I say, "but I happen to think they're pretty funny."

"Oh, sure, funny for you. You don't have to babysit them tonight and listen to them try to sing hardcore rap while playing *Call of Duty* at full volume."

"Poor you," I say.

We head toward the escalators and I think we're on our way out of the mall, but instead, she pulls me down a different path from our usual route.

"Where are we going?" I ask.

"You'll see," she says as she leads me into CVS.

"What, do you need tampons or something?" I ask.

"Nope."

I can't imagine what she's up to, but she seems to know exactly where she's going. Her precision maneuvering through aisles toward the back of the store leads us straight to the condom selection.

"No way!" I practically squeal.

"You can't be too prepared," Danielle says with mock seriousness.

We browse through the multitude of choices: Lubricated, Sensitivity, Ecstasy, Ultra Smooth, Fire and Ice, Ribbed, and the Midnight Collection, whatever that is. My head is spinning. Could they possibly be that different from one another? Is there a right or wrong answer? I wonder if Luke has a favorite. What if I pick the worst one?

Danielle tells me that she and Charlie have tried almost all of them, and the ribbed is definitely their go-to choice.

"Isn't the guy supposed to take care of this?" I ask.

"Of course. And I'm sure Luke has a drawer full of them."

Ouch. The thought of Luke with a stockpile of condoms makes me wince. I hate the idea that he's been with other girls. "Then why are we here?" I ask, genuinely confused.

"Because if you show up with protection, he'll know that you're ready. He won't worry that he's somehow pushing you into something. And trust me, it'll be the biggest turn-on ever."

"Makes sense," I say, browsing through the buffet of prophylactics. "Do they go bad? I mean, what if I'm not ready for a while and they sit in my dresser for six months?"

"First of all," Danielle says as though she's talking to a small child, "Luke will be gone in six months. Second of all, don't be naive."

I'm not sure if I'm being naive because I wonder if condoms somehow expire or if it's because I think I might want to wait what is evidently way too long. Hearing Danielle say that Luke will be gone is a painful reminder of our limited time together. The thought is always looming in my mind somewhere, but hearing someone else say it out loud is a reality check. I guess I have to make the most of the little time we have left.

"You know the first time is going to hurt, right?" Danielle asks.

"Yeah, I guess," I say.

"It really hurts," she says, looking at me grimly.

"Really?" I ask, trying to gauge the level of pain she's describing.

"Well, it's different for every girl. But I swear, it *does* get better."

"It's got to, right? Or else everyone wouldn't be talking about it," I say, trying to focus on the positive. We share a giggle and I turn my attention back to the display. I grab an assortment of colored packages. Danielle gets an economy pack of Ultra Ribbed in a bright gold box.

"I'm going over to Charlie's to put these to good use before I have to babysit the monsters," Danielle says as we exit the store. "I'll drive you home."

"TMI, Dani," I say with a cringe. "I don't need a play-by-play." This moment is one where, if Sloan were here, she would chime in, and we'd both give Danielle grief about her tendency to overshare. I hate that Sloan's not here to offer her advice and comic relief. How long are we going to go without talking? Is it up to me to repair this rift? I don't think I've done anything wrong, but Sloan is infinitely more stubborn than I am, and she could stay silent for god knows how long.

I walk into my house to find my mom in the kitchen unloading groceries. She always does a big Friday-afternoon shopping trip so we have snacks and fresh fruit for the weekend. Since she's in the classroom all week, she puts on her mom hat on Fridays at four, which means homemade cookies in the afternoon, fresh-squeezed orange juice on Saturday and Sunday mornings, and usually some big dish like lasagna or chili that we dig into all weekend long.

I try to walk past the kitchen. No such luck.

"Come say hi," Mom calls.

Before I walk into the kitchen, I plop my stuff by the front door. I fear that with her x-ray vision, she will see the condoms through the thick leather of my purse. "Hi, Mom," I say and give her a kiss on the cheek. "What smells so good?"

"Baked ziti."

"Yum. My fave."

"You around tonight?" she asks.

"Yeah, but I need to run a quick errand. Okay to take your car?"

"Sure. Key's on the hook."

"Thanks, love you," I say as I grab my purse and snag the key from the hook by the front door.

Less than ten minutes later, I pull up in front of Sloan's house. I have been practicing my strategy and making-up dialogue in my head, but now I'm too scared to get out of the car. My heart is pounding and my mouth is dry. I grab a piece of gum and make myself walk up to the door and ring the bell.

Gabby, Sloan's oldest sister, opens the door while typing something on her phone. Without even glancing up at me, she says, "She's in the den."

I walk back to the den, where Sloan is lying on the sofa with the television on and a bag of Cheeto Puffs in her lap. She looks up and tries her best to hide how surprised she is to see me.

"Hi," I say.

"Hi," she says, giving nothing away. She's not going to make this easy on me.

"I miss you," I say.

"You do?" she asks.

"Yeah, a lot."

"Okay," she says, but she doesn't offer anything else. No *I miss you, too,* or *Thanks for coming over.*

I recite the words I rehearsed in the car. "I just want to

tell you that you're too important to me to lose you over a boy. I think there's room for both you and Luke in my life, and I hope we can figure this out."

"Okay," she says again. I can't tell if her voice is softening. Stubborn to the core.

I stand there uncomfortably for what feels like an eternity, but in essence, it's probably just ten or twenty seconds. Finally I turn to leave.

"Wait," she says. I turn around. "I'm really embarrassed."

"What are you embarrassed about?" I ask.

"Please, Janey. I acted like such a bitch, and I don't know why. I'm happy for you, I really am. I don't know what my problem is. I'm so sorry. I'm the one who should be making the effort here, not you." I can see that her eyes are getting glassy, and she swallows audibly, as though she's trying to push down the lump rising in her throat.

I plop down next to her on the sofa and hug her tight. She hugs back and I instantly begin to cry.

"All this stuff with Luke is a big deal," I say through sniffles, "and it sucks that I can't share it with you."

"You *can* share it with me," she sniffles back. "Please, I want you to. I want to hear everything."

"You do?"

"Yes," she says. Then she pulls away so she can look me in the eye. "Is there something I need to know?"

"I bought condoms!" I whisper in her ear.

"What?!" she screams.

"I bought condoms without you and I hated it. I need you, Sloan. And not just for condom shopping."

"Well, it's not like I'm the condom connoisseur," she says.

"Oh, come on. I bet you know what to get even though you've never used one."

"Yeah," she says, "that's probably true."

I open my purse and spill out the collection of rubbers. We laugh and cry as the drama and anger of the last four days slip away. We go into her room because Sloan wants to show me a new dress she bought that she wants me to borrow for my next date with Luke. It's pale gray and short with long sleeves and a deep scooped neck.

"Try it on," she insists.

I do as she instructs and love the dress. Even though Sloan and I have different bodies—she is a little shorter and much curvier than I am—we can often share clothes because she likes things to hug her body and I prefer my clothes less revealing.

"This dress is so good," I say with genuine enthusiasm.

She snaps a photo me with her phone. "OMG, you look amazing. Should we post it on Instagram? Or not, because we don't want Luke to get a preview before he sees it in person."

"I don't follow him on Insta. I'm not even sure if he has an account," I say.

"What? You don't follow each other?" she asks, incredulous.

"He never requested, and I didn't want to seem like a creeper."

"You never searched him?" she asks, looking at me like I'm crazy.

"No. I told you, I didn't want to stalk."

"Well, you know me, I have no trouble stalking." Sloan goes on Instagram and searches *Luke Hallstrom*. His account comes up. He only has about ten pictures posted: some of him on the track and at meets with his buddies, one of his whole family all dressed up, but of course the two pictures I zero in on are the ones of him with Amanda. One is clearly a selfie where they're laughing, wearing matching La Jolla High baseball hats. The other photo is from a formal or prom or something, and they look annoyingly perfect. I hate seeing it. And I hate that I hate it.

"Why are those still up?" I ask.

"He probably never thought to remove them," Sloan assures me. "Guys don't think about that stuff. And anyway, it's not like they had an ugly breakup or anything, right?"

"No, of course not," I say with slight sarcasm. "Luke loves everyone and everyone loves Luke."

"Hey, hey," Sloan soothes. "You're the one he's with now. You're the one he wants."

"I know," I say, taking a deep breath, trying to inhale some sanity. "Ugh! Why is it that being in a relationship makes me feel so insecure? It should have the opposite effect. It's counterintuitive."

"Don't worry. Anyone can see that he's crazy for you."

Just then, my phone makes the *pong* sound, letting me know I've just gotten a text. I pull it from my back pocket. The text is from Luke: *Miss ya.* I show it to Sloan. We both bust up laughing. It's so nice to have her back.

CHAPTER TWENTY-ONE

IT'S SATURDAY EVENING and I'm going to Luke's house for dinner. His mom is cooking, and it's just going to be Luke, his parents, and me. I'm beyond nervous. It feels so official and daunting. Luke is acting like it's no big deal. We were texting while I was at Sloan's and he wrote, *Wanna come over for dinner tomorrow?* Sloan and I thought for sure that meant that his parents would be out and he and I would get some delicious takeout and curl up on the sofa, for starters.

Sure. Sounds good, I responded.

Great. My mom's making steak. You eat red meat, right? I showed my phone to Sloan, and the laughter that started when I got that first text from Luke escalated into full hysterics.

Now here I am in my mom's car on the way to his house, wondering what the hell I'm doing. What are we going to talk about? What are they going to ask me? Did he have his other girlfriends over for dinner? Is this some kind of screening process? Am I dressed appropriately?

I'm wearing Sloan's gray dress (a sure sign your friend is true blue is that she lets you wear her brand-new clothes even before she does). I have a bouquet of daisies on the passenger seat, which my mom picked up at the farmers' market. "You never show up at someone's house empty-handed," she repeats every time we are guests in someone's home. My mom also told me to make sure to offer to help in the kitchen and to clear the dishes. As if I didn't know.

I ring the doorbell and Luke answers the door instantly. He's in jeans and a black cashmere sweater. He looks utterly edible.

"That's so cute," he says. "You got all dressed up." Now I feel ridiculous. How was I supposed to know the dress code for these things? "Come on in."

Luke takes my hand and guides me into the living room, which is decorated with green plaid wallpaper and red leather club chairs. His parents are sitting on a plush green velvet sofa by the fireplace, each holding a glass of red wine in an oversize goblet. They stand up when we walk in the room and I am relieved to see that his mom is also wearing a dress. Granted, hers is purple, and the crisp fabric makes her look like the First Lady, but maybe the fact that I'm also in a dress will make her think I'm respectful.

Mr. and Mrs. Hallstrom are older than my parents, making them appear serious and slightly intimidating. I remind myself that Luke is eighteen and the youngest of three kids, so of course his mom and dad would be older. His dad is silver-haired and handsome in his V-neck red sweater and gray slacks. His mom has dark hair, and she's pretty in a country club sort of way. She wears bright red lipstick and simple, expensive-looking jewelry.

After a few minutes of formal small talk, Mrs. Hallstrom says she's going to go check on dinner. I immediately stand up, my mother's voice in my head, and ask, "Can I do anything to help?"

"No, sweetheart, we're all set," she responds with genuine appreciation.

At dinner, Mr. and Mrs. Hallstrom sit at opposite ends of a rectangular table. Luke and I sit next to each other on one side. Monica, their housekeeper, serves dinner; however, it is made abundantly clear that Mrs. Hallstrom did the cooking. Even though the rare flank steak, roasted red potatoes, and sautéed green beans look delicious, I have no appetite. My hands fidget in my lap. Why am I so nervous?

Mr. Hallstrom looks at me with interest. "Janey, tell us about your family."

Is this where I tell them that my parents are separated? Does that make me damaged goods? I guess I can't leave it out. They probably don't want their untarnished son to end up with someone from a broken home, but they're bound to find out soon enough. I figure I'll start with the good stuff and end with the bad news. "I'm an only child, and I'm very close to my mom and dad. My dad's a commercial airline pilot, and my mom teaches kindergarten."

"How nice," Mrs. Hallstrom says. "I'm an only child, and my parents were my best friends. The three of us were always together when I was growing up. Lovely that you have that, too."

Crap. Guess I waited too long to drop the bomb. "They're newly separated," I say quickly to get it over with. "We're all just figuring it out."

"I'm sorry to hear that," Mr. Hallstrom says. And then there's silence, long silence wherein I assume they're figuring Luke could do much better. "Darling, more wine?" Mr. Hallstrom asks his wife as he lifts the bottle.

"I'll have some," Luke says, seemingly well aware of how his parents will react.

"Hilarious," Mr. Hallstrom says dryly. "You can have wine when you're twenty-one. Just three short years away."

"You know, there's talk that California's drinking age is going to be lowered to eighteen," Luke offers.

"Well," Mrs. Hallstrom adds, "as soon as it's the law, you may have a glass of wine at our dinner table."

"I debated that topic," I chime in.

"Oh? You're on the debate team?" I wonder if Luke told his parents anything about me.

"Yes, since middle school."

"Janey's a total star," Luke announces.

"What side of the debate did you argue?" his dad wants to know.

"I had prop," I say, and then I realize that might not be clear. "Proposition."

"Which means you made a case to lower the drinking age?"

"Yes, but we have to prepare both sides, because we don't know until right before which we'll be assigned."

"And did you win that round?" Mrs. Hallstrom wants to know.

"I think I might have," I say with as much modesty as possible.

"Tell me the strongest argument in favor of lowering the drinking age," Mr. Hallstrom says with interest.

Really? He wants me to recite my argument? I guess I can tell him the data without the passion and fervor I use when actually debating. "Um. Well. Eighteen- to twenty-year-olds, who fall below the legal drinking age, tend to partake in binge drinking when they consume alcoholic beverages." All of a sudden, I feel more self-assured, like I have something to contribute to the conversation other than talk of my sad family situation.

"That makes a certain amount of sense," Mr. Hallstrom concedes. "But it stands to reason that more drinking at a young age will only lead to more addiction and accidents. Also, drinking at a younger age has got to affect brain development, doesn't it?"

"Well," I counter, "there is evidence that prohibiting

alcohol consumption for people in this age group in public places makes them drink in unsupervised places, which makes them more vulnerable to negative consequences of underage drinking. Therefore, if the age is lowered to eighteen, they will get to drink in moderation, without the worry of breaking the law." I realize that my language sounds very official, and that in normal conversation I wouldn't speak so formally, but because I've written and rewritten the arguments and read them and recited them so many times, it becomes a script that I have committed to memory

"Fascinating," Mrs. Hallstrom says, and it seems she really means it.

Luke grabs my hand under the table and gives it a little squeeze. My whole body relaxes and I feel like maybe I belong at this table.

Dessert is apple pie with gourmet vanilla ice cream and Luke whines a little bit because he thought his mom was making a red velvet cake, his favorite. Mrs. Hallstrom seems sincerely apologetic that she disappointed him.

"The Granny Smith apples were just too gorgeous to resist," she explains.

"I think I'll survive," Luke says in a tiny, sad voice that elicits a giggle from his parents. It's obvious they think he hung the moon. Their baby. The divine third child.

I don't want to overstay my welcome, and I'm not sure how long these things are supposed to last, so after I help clear the dishes, I thank his parents for dinner and claim that I have to get home to get some work done. Luke walks me out to my mom's car, which I parked in front of their next-door neighbor's house because Luke's Jeep is parked in front of his house.

Before I open the driver's-side door, Luke presses me up against the car with every part of his body. Paranoid, I look up to see if his parents might be spying on us from their window. Thankfully, there is a big hedge separating the two homes and hiding us from all potentially curious eyes.

"You were awesome," he whispers, practically into my mouth. "I can tell my parents really like you."

"Really?" I want to hear it again. I want to know that his parents approve.

"Big time." He leans in hungrily and kisses me full on the lips.

My eyes close, my arms wrap around him, and I feel wetness between my legs the second his tongue enters my mouth. As soon as he's near me, touching me, kissing me, my body responds automatically. I feel weak, I moan, I get wet. I am physiologically connected to this guy, and it's clear my body wants him desperately. I want to have sex with him. Every organ I possess is telling me that I want to have sex with him. On second thought, it might be more of a need. I need to have sex with him. The same way I need food, water, and shelter.

He must sense my physical responses to him because he starts breathing deeper, pressing with more urgency. I feel his erection against my pelvis. It's so hard and hot. The heat makes me sweat. My insides are on fire.

Is it possible that seven minutes ago I was helping with dishes in his mother's kitchen and now I'm feeling her son's boner practically tearing a hole in Sloan's dress?

CHAPTER TWENTY-TWO

IDRIVE HOME SMILING. I cannot stop smiling. I wonder: If another driver pulled up next to me, what would he think is going on in my car or in my brain? This goofy grin is plastered across my face, and I can't wipe it off no matter how hard I try. The car practically drives itself home, and I float into the house to find my mom sitting in the living room. She's sitting straight up on the love seat, not watching television, not reading, not doing a crossword puzzle or playing Words with Friends. She's just sitting and staring.

"Hi," I say, cautiously awaiting bad news.

"Hello, Janey," she says with a serious edge to her voice.

"What's up?"

"I found your condoms," she says. No lead-in. No *Honey, we need to talk.* Just *I found your condoms.* And something about the *your* is so piercing and accusatory. She could have said *the* condoms. She put a particular emphasis on the *your,* as if they were engraved with my initials, making them especially revolting.

Then it occurs to me that I put the condoms way down deep in my bathing-suit drawer, under a one-piece bathing suit I had to use for PE in middle school. I wonder what my mom was doing looking through that drawer. Was she snooping? What was she hoping to find?

"Were you searching my room?"

"Let's focus on the issue at hand, shall we?" she says.

I hate when parents do that. They deflect the part of the scenario where they might be guilty. They get so busy throwing their anger and disappointment around, but always find a way to bury the things they've done wrong. Don't I deserve some privacy? Isn't it *my* room? I'm a good, trustworthy kid, and I don't think she should be snooping around in the depths of my drawers if I haven't given her any reason to suspect I'm breaking any laws.

I guess that's the point here. She *did* suspect something. She went looking for evidence that I was keeping secrets from her. I'm seventeen, and I'm falling crazy, madly in love with a boy. Am I a criminal for considering having sex with him? Was I supposed to ask her permission? I'm willing to bet my mom didn't get anyone's permission the first time she had sex. In effect, didn't I do the right thing by taking the matter into my own hands to ensure I was protected from disease and pregnancy? I should be complimented for being so responsible. She should be singing my praises for my careful planning and forethought.

"I haven't done anything," I say.

"What do you mean by *anything?*" she asks.

"I haven't had sex."

"Good. You've known this guy ten minutes. Am I supposed to be proud of you for waiting this long?" Her voice registers her disgust.

"Mom, why are you freaking out?"

"Why am I freaking out? Maybe because my daughter has a couple of dates and seems to be in a big hurry to give her virginity away. I don't think you're ready. You've never even dated before. How do you know this is the right guy?"

"It's not easy to talk to you when you're so angry and irrational," I say.

Mom seems to actually listen to my plea. She takes a deep breath. One thing my mom has always been good at is admitting when she's wrong. Whenever she's raised her voice to me, which has not been often at all, she's always apologized.

"I'm just worried about you. This is all new territory. For both of us. I'm not sure how to navigate it," she explains.

"I'm sorry you're worried. I'm not going to rush into anything. You've always trusted me, and I haven't changed. I'm still the same girl who has earned your trust," I say.

"Maybe you haven't had sex yet, but clearly you're thinking about it," she says, searching for answers. "So you're not that far off."

I don't know what she wants to hear. Does she expect me to tell her exactly how far we've gone? Forget it. Sure, she and I have a close relationship, but she's still my mother, and I don't think any mother really wants or needs to hear her daughter's plans for her first time. "I'm not ready to have this conversation," I say softly, trying not to offend her or get her back into her angry state.

"Then you're not ready to do it," she says in a quiet but firm voice.

"I don't think those two things are connected," I say, bracing myself for the fury.

"You're wrong."

"Just because I don't want to discuss details with my mother means I'm too immature to have sex?"

"Yes, as a matter of fact. Sex brings an unexpected set of complications and risks to your life. You have to be able to acknowledge those factors and discuss them like an adult."

"I know those things and I can discuss those things. Just . . ."

"Not with me?" she asks, sounding wounded.

"Correct."

"I didn't think we kept things from each other."

"Mom, I think you're being a little unrealistic."

"Would you talk about it with your father?" There it is. The first time she said *your father,* instead of *Dad.* I've always noticed that married people talk to their kids about each other using *Mom* or *Mommy* and *Dad* or *Daddy,* which has a warm, inclusive meaning, as though they all share one another. *Your father* implies that he's only mine, that his role as father no longer includes her.

I probably wouldn't talk about my readiness for sex with my dad. But I really don't think he would've attacked me this way if he had he found the condoms. Although he would also never go digging though my drawers in search of signs that I've been a bad girl. I really miss my dad right now. If nothing else, he would provide perspective and be able to talk my mom out of her hysteria. He could always put a gentle hand on her shoulder when she got anxious or worked up, and it seemed to have the magical power to calm her and restore sanity. My mother watches me process my thoughts as if she can read my mind.

"Would you?" she presses.

"I don't know, but I wish he were here."

My mom closes her eyes and swallows audibly, suggesting she's trying to keep the tears from flowing. She stands up and walks into her room. She doesn't stomp or huff or slam the door. But I do hear the gentle click of her bedroom door being closed, signifying a deep chasm between us. I feel so alone. My house is quiet and sad. The house that used to be inhabited by a family is now a place where my mom refers to the man who used to be her soul mate as *your father* and I sit alone in the living room wishing I could fix this mess.

CHAPTER TWENTY-THREE

VALENTINE'S DAY IS ALMOST HERE. I've never had a boyfriend on Valentine's Day, and I've always thought Valentine's Day was reserved for those doting couples that I would never be half of. Unlike some girls, I never really cared. Now that it's almost here, I don't know what I'm supposed to do. Naturally, I ask my friends.

"Valentine's Day is for girls. He is supposed to make the grand gesture. You're supposed to do nothing except have him treat you like a queen," Sloan offers.

"That is the worst advice ever," I say.

"It's true," she protests.

"It's kinda true," Danielle chimes in as we sit outside the cafeteria during a break between classes. "You do something sweet and thoughtful, he does jewelry."

"Jewelry? Are you crazy?" I ask in disbelief. "We've been dating for six weeks. We haven't even had sex. Why would he get me jewelry?"

Sloan shakes her head as if she's baffled by my

ignorance. "He gets you jewelry so you'll *want* to have sex with him." Danielle laughs in what appears to be agreement.

"Have you met me?" I ask. "That's not how I operate."

"Just do something simple and nice, and let him take care of the rest," Danielle says. "Has he asked you out for Valentine's Day?"

"Yes. His parents are going to be out of town, and we're going to hang out at his house."

"Oh, that's huge!" squeaks Sloan. "Do you think it's gonna happen?"

"I don't know. I'm not sure I'm ready," I say.

"Bring the condoms just in case," advises Danielle.

"Yeah," agrees Sloan. "That jewelry might be very expensive."

"E.B.!" I yell as I throw the rest of my granola bar at her.

The day before Valentine's Day, I'm in the kitchen making two dozen red velvet cupcakes for Luke's Valentine's Day gift. I remember from dinner at his house that red velvet is his favorite. A gift of baked goods adheres to Danielle's advice in that it's thoughtful, and frankly I just couldn't think of anything else. Although I do wonder what he's going to do with twenty-four cupcakes . . .

I happen to love baking. My mom and I always baked when I was little. My favorite was white cake out of the box with white icing made from powdered sugar, butter, and vanilla extract.

I hear my mom's car in the driveway. Things have been a little frosty between us since she found the condoms. Strangely, she didn't confiscate them. After our fight, I checked my drawer and was surprised to see that they were right where I left them. Right where she uncovered them. I guess I could have taken them out and left them on my desk or the kitchen counter in plain view. After all, both people who live in this house know the condoms are staying here with us. But it seems appropriate to leave them buried, as if they're still worthy of a secret.

Mom comes into the kitchen. "Whatcha making?"

"Red velvet cupcakes."

"Nice. For Luke?"

"Yes, for Valentine's Day."

"Perfect gift," she says. "Need any help?"

"No, I think I've got it," I say.

She gives me a little kiss on the forehead and leaves the kitchen. Two seconds later, she's back.

"I hate this," she says. "I love you. Here you are, going through a very important time in your life, and I want you to know that I'm on your side."

"Thanks, Mom. I love you too."

"I also want you to know that I trust you. I know you're a good kid with a good head on your shoulders, and I believe you'll do what's right for you."

"Oh, Mommy," I say, putting down the sifter. "That means so much to me." I give my mom a hug. A big, strong, long-overdue hug. We hug for a while, neither of us wanting to be the first to let go.

"Use an ice cream scooper," she whispers in my ear.

I pull away. "What?" I ask. Is my mother giving me some kinky sex tip?

"To fill the cupcake liners. If you use an ice cream scooper, all the cupcakes will be the same size." Phew.

Luke's parents are spending a long weekend in Massachusetts and Luke has the house to himself. When I asked him who was staying with him, he practically laughed in my face.

"I'm eighteen," he reminded me.

"I know. But you're still a kid," I said. I just couldn't imagine being left in the house alone for four days. What if there was a fire or a gas leak or an earthquake?

"I'm pretty sure I'll be just fine, but thanks for worrying about me. If you want to sleep over and keep me safe, you're more than welcome," he says.

"Yeah, right. I'm sure that would go over big with my mom," I said.

I've been counting the minutes until our Valentine's Day dinner. I told him I had dessert covered, so he said he'd take care of the main course. I debated whether to bring a condom. Sloan said if I have it, I'm more likely to use it, and if I don't bring it, there's a better chance I won't agree to have sex with him. She says if she really doesn't want to go too far with a guy, but is worried she might be tempted, she won't shave down there—that way she knows she won't let him take her pants off. Good policy, I suppose. But, in the end, I put a condom in my purse.

I walk up to his house holding two large trays of the red velvet cupcakes with cream cheese frosting. My mom's ice cream scooper trick worked perfectly. She also picked up red sugar sprinkles to dust over the icing, making them look extra special and sort of professional.

Luke opens the door looking particularly gorgeous and irresistible. His hair is still a little wet, giving me an instant mental image of him in a recent shower. I haven't even stepped into his foyer and I'm already picturing him naked. My body immediately goes weak and gooey. He leans in to kiss me and I smell his shampoo and his soap and his minty breath. I love that he got ready for me.

"Red velvet?" he asks excitedly as we walk to his kitchen and I place the trays on the center island.

"Yup!" I say.

"You remembered," he says.

"Of course," I say. "Happy Valentine's Day."

"Please don't make me wait," he says, reaching for one of the cupcakes.

"Go for it," I say, honored that my cupcakes look so good that he feels compelled try them immediately.

He removes a cupcake from the corner of the tray and takes a giant bite. He moans exaggeratedly with great pleasure. He has a huge dollop of cream cheese frosting right in the center of his upper lip. There's no way he can't feel it. I watch him with a big smile on my face, wondering whether he's going to wipe that frosting off or lick it. For now, he does nothing except shove the rest of the cupcake into his mouth, leaving even more frosting on his face.

I watch him chew and swallow with his eyes closed, as if he's in complete ecstasy. Finally, he opens his eyes.

"Incredible," he says. I'm staring at his frosting-covered face, trying not to laugh.

"What?" he asks, feigning ignorance. I continue to stare. "What?" he asks again. "Do I have something on my face?"

I nod.

"Come lick it off," he says, pulling me into his arms and kissing me while deliberately transferring the frosting from his face onto mine. Our tongues intertwine, and we lick the inside and outside of each other's mouths. "The only thing that tastes better than your cupcake is you," he says.

He lifts me up and sits me on the island, his lips still on mine. He stands between my legs, leaning against me. I take hold of his hands and finger the leather strap around his wrist. His lips leave my mouth and work their way down my neck. My head falls back in sheer bliss as he finds his way to my chest. Somehow he simultaneously unbuttons my shirt and kisses my chest. I wonder where he picked up these advanced skills. Before I know it, my shirt is off and I'm sitting on his mother's kitchen island in my leggings and bra.

"Is it okay with you if we have dinner later?" he asks, a little breathless.

"Sure," I say.

He helps me off the island and guides me into his backyard. We walk through French doors to a covered patio. On the left is a big grassy lawn and to the right is a long rectangular pool joined at the back by a hot tub that is radiating steam as if it's welcoming us into its bubbly water.

"Want to go in the hot tub?" he asks.

"I didn't bring a bathing suit," I say. The words sound silly and naive and I know it.

"That's okay," he says. "I didn't either." He unbuttons his jeans, slides them off his hips, and lets them fall to the brick patio. He then whips his shirt over his head and drops it on top of his crumpled jeans. He stands there in his boxer briefs, a huge erection poking at the cotton, begging to be released. I look at his beautiful body, marveling at his ability to stand there, looking at me, without the slightest hint of self-consciousness. "You're overdressed," he says.

I tuck my fingertips into the waistband of my leggings and slowly push them down the length of my legs. He watches me, his eyes moving from my eyes to my body, which is gradually revealing itself to him. He turns me around gently, then unhooks my bra and lets it fall next to all the other discarded clothing. We've been in this position before, both in our underwear, but I know it's not stopping here tonight. He takes my hand and leads me over to the hot tub. The jets are already on, making me realize he has a plan in mind and in place. I do love a man with a plan.

He tucks a fingertip into my underwear at one hip and gently strokes my skin inside the waistband across my belly to the other hip.

"I want to take these off. Is that okay?" he asks quietly, carefully.

"Yes." The word is barely audible, a cautious whisper.

"Was that a yes?" he asks.

"Yes," I say, turning up volume slightly.

With both hands, he slides my lacy black underwear down my legs. As if he knows it wouldn't be fair for only one of us to be naked, he takes his own underwear off immediately. There we are, totally naked. Am I supposed to look at his penis? Touch it? I glance at it fleetingly and find that it looks exactly how it's supposed to look. I look back up at him and catch his stare.

My instincts are to close my eyes really tight and jump into the pool to submerge my nudity under the darkness of the water, but Luke grabs my hands and takes a long, adoring look at my body.

"Perfection," he whispers.

Just weeks ago, I could barely look at myself in the

mirror in shorts and a T-shirt without feeling a pang of disappointment at the perceived mediocrity that stared back at me. I always saw myself as so far beneath the category of pretty, feminine, or sexy, let alone *perfect*. And here I am, completely naked, and the most handsome guy I know seems to be in awe of what he sees. How is it that I never saw myself the way he sees me? Why is it that I needed him to open that door for me? I don't want to be the kind of girl who needs validation from boys. I don't want to believe I'm beautiful just because he tells me it's true. However, I am grateful to him for giving me the tools to shed my self-doubt. Because of Luke, I believe that I don't need to look like the leggy, curvy girls in the locker room to feel attractive. I allow him to stare at me, and it makes me feel positively sexy.

He guides me into the steamy water of the hot tub. He sits on the bench in the water and pulls me onto his lap, facing him. I feel his hardness between my legs. His hands are wrapped around my back, and mine are around his neck. He kisses me more deeply and passionately than ever before, if that's even possible. His hands move down my back and explore my butt and my waist as he pulls me closer to him, pushing me against him. The kissing is constant, while I drop my hands to feel him. It's smooth and the skin is soft, but the whole thing is so incredibly hard, much harder than I would have thought possible. It turns me on even more to touch it, and the worry that I wouldn't know what to do with it immediately vanishes.

It's instinctual to stroke it and feel it and explore it. His breathing gets heavier, which tells me that I'm probably doing it right. He stops kissing me and leans his head back against the brick in a clear display of rapture. I love knowing I'm making him feel good.

He shifts my body up a bit so that he is poking me, a gentle knock on a door, hoping to be let in. My heart stops. I feel panic. I'm scared. Every inch of my body freezes. I'm not ready. Something must have changed in my rhythm, because he opens his eyes to look at me.

"You okay?" he asks breathlessly.

"I'm not ready," I blurt. The words reverberate in my head and I'm worried that I sound like a little girl who's not ready to have her first sleepover or go on her first roller coaster.

"That's okay," he says sweetly, kissing me on the lips. Once. Twice. Three times.

"I'm sorry," I say.

"You don't have to be sorry," he says. "I'm a very patient person." I am mortified. I feel small and immature. I should have thought this through. Is this what boys call being a tease? I'm such an idiot. I think he can tell that I feel awful. "Hey," he says, grabbing my hand under the water. "It's okay. Don't worry."

"Really?" I ask. "You sure?"

"Yes, it's okay. I'm not in a hurry."

"I don't want to disappoint you," I say.

"You're far from a disappointment," he says. "You're the best. I really like you."

"You do?"

"Of course I do. I like you so much. This is not about how quickly I can have sex with you."

"Okay," I say. "But I still feel bad."

"Don't," he says. "I'm really happy with everything that is happening right now." He kisses me on the lips as if to accentuate his point. "I don't know about you, but I'm starving."

"Starving," I concur.

"I'll grab us some towels," Luke says. He jumps out of the hot tub and goes to the lounge, where two fluffy gray towels are folded into neat squares. His wet, muscular body glimmers in the moonlight. He twists one towel around his waist and brings a second one over to the hot tub and holds it out for me. I step out of the water and he wraps me up in the towel with a warm squeeze.

Twenty minutes later, I'm wearing a pair of Luke's La Jolla High Track sweatpants and a Boston College sweatshirt. We're sitting on the floor in his den eating Thai takeout from the boxes and talking about our favorite music. Luke is into classic rock: U2, Springsteen, The Who, Led Zeppelin, and other bands my dad always listens to. Somehow that music seems infinitely cooler now that I know Luke likes it. I guess I owe my dad an apology for all the eye

rolling I've given him for his love of music from the seventies and eighties. With embarrassment, I admit to Luke
that I still know all the words to the songs from the
High School Musical movies. He doesn't seem to hold it
against me.

After dinner, we head into the kitchen to throw the
food cartons away and put the forks in the dishwasher. I
take the cover off of one of the trays of cupcakes.

"I need another one," he says, picking up a cupcake.
"I'll probably end up eating all of these."

"You're supposed to," I say. "They're your Valentine's
Day present."

"Oh, that reminds me," he says. "Be right back."

Luke leaves the kitchen and returns momentarily with
a little black box in one hand and a card in the other. It
makes me nervous. I feel like I don't deserve whatever is
in that little black box.

I fetch the card I have for him from my purse. It never
took me so long to choose a card as it took to choose this
one. I stood in the aisle at the Hallmark store for forty-
five minutes, looking at every option and then going back
to reread ones I'd already discounted. I didn't know how
serious or sentimental to be. I found a simple red card
with one pink heart on the front. The print on the inside reads *Be Mine*. Underneath the print, I wrote: *Dear
Luke, Thank you for making this the best Valentine's Day ever.
I'm having a great time hanging out with you. I hope you enjoy
the cupcakes. xoxo Janey.* The wording took me even lon-

ger than the card selection. We have never used the word *love,* so I don't want to be the first to throw it out there. I couldn't even bring myself to write *I love hanging out with you.* Sloan and Danielle confirmed that I was taking the right approach. I felt good about what I wrote. Until now.

He hands me his card along with the box and I give him my card. We open our cards simultaneously. The front of the card he chose has a picture of two puppies with their noses pressed together. The preprinted part inside reads: *Every day is Valentine's Day when I'm with you.* In his boyish scrawl he wrote: *It's very true. Love, Luke.* He wasn't afraid to use the word *love.* Is the boy supposed to say it first?

"Open your present," he says, taking a big bite of a cupcake. I take the red ribbon off the box and lift the lid. Inside is a delicate gold bracelet with a tiny gold heart. It's gorgeous and I love it more than anything else I have ever owned.

"This is beautiful. Wow, Luke, I don't know what to say." I've never gotten jewelry from a boy before, and I can't find the right words to string together.

"I'm glad you like it."

I take it out of the box and put it on my wrist. The shiny gold heart rests against my skin and glints in the light of the overhead lamp. "I love it."

"Good," he says and gives me a kiss. He pulls away after a quick little peck, but I grab him and pull him in for a longer, more passionate kiss.

I have put the responsibility of every step of this romance in Luke's hands. He has initiated every plan and every kiss, and he wrote *love* on his card when I was too chicken. It's time I show him that I can jump in with both feet.

"I love the bracelet," I say softly. My heart races. I'm terrified, but I'm determined to say it. "And I love you."

He looks at me as though I've taken him by complete surprise. "You do?" he asks.

"Yep," I say, trying to sound more self-possessed than I feel.

"Good."

"Good?" I ask. Is that the appropriate response here? "That's all you have to say?"

"Very good," he says, a tiny smirk creeping across his lips. Is he toying with me?

"Very good," I repeat in near disbelief.

"Yes, Janey, that's very good news. Because I love you too."

"You do?" I ask.

"Yep," he says. Our conversation is now repeating itself in reverse.

"Good," I tease.

"Good? That's all you have to say?" he asks in mock surprise.

"Very good," I say, smiling.

CHAPTER TWENTY-FOUR

THERE'S A PRESEASON TRACK MEET at Escondido High School, and Coach Chow is acting like it's the Olympic trials. Luke and I are sitting toward the back of the bus. Luke brought an extra pair of earbuds and a splitter so he can educate me about the art of letting Bono and The Edge get me amped for the meet. We sit close, holding hands, our heads tilted toward each other. I think the other people on the track team are now used to seeing us together, so we no longer get curious stares or chuckles, like we're being caught in the act. Every once in a while, though, I notice a longing glance from another girl on the team that seems to translate to: *Aw, you guys are sooooo cute.*

This is the first track meet that will not be attended by at least one of my parents. Typically, they show up at everything. Long after other high school kids' parents stopped dragging themselves to debates, mine would be there. I had to beg them to stop coming with the promise that I would share all the details upon my return. I'm only a little surprised they don't have me wired so they can play back every round. Same thing for track meets. They've always come to all my meets, including preseason matchups that mean nothing. I downplayed this one in an effort to keep them away. I didn't even call it a meet. I just said we were going to have a scrimmage-type workout against another high school. They bought it. Maybe they're starting to get the picture. It's my first meet since I've started dating Luke, and I want to do especially well, not only to impress him, but to show myself that I am not distracted by my boyfriend. I want the peace of mind of knowing that being in a relationship is not getting in the way of my success.

The meet is awesome. I am focused, fast, and light on my feet. Maybe it's the extra time I've put in at optional workouts. Maybe it's all the stretching I've done in the last couple of weeks with the sole intent of lingering, waiting for Luke to finish his high jumps. Maybe it's the brilliant lyrics of U2 still ringing in my ears: *What you don't have you don't need it now. What you don't know you can feel it somehow.* I end up taking first place in the mile and the 300-meter low hurdles. Both times, I can hear Luke cheering me on. My relay team takes second place, which is a huge accomplishment since it's a new team, only recently assembled by Coach Chow. This is the first time the four of us have run together, which means when we get used to one another's rhythms, we'll be unstoppable.

I watch Luke's high jump, long jump, and 100-yard dash. I love watching him race. He is a fierce competitor, like he is going into battle every time he hears the gun. And every time, he absolutely eviscerates the enemy.

Our team does very well, and I even catch Coach Chow cracking a smile or two. The regular season looks promising.

At the end of the meet, everyone is packing up their belongings, changing their shoes, and saying goodbye to friends and acquaintances from other schools. I know my parents are curious to hear how it went, so I take my phone from my bag and see that, indeed, they texted me several times asking for updates. I sit on a bench and respond to them with a few highlights. When I look up from my phone I see a gorgeous, statuesque girl wearing an Escondido High School track uniform talking to Luke. Her long blond ponytail sways over her shoulders as she laughs animatedly about something apparently hilarious that Luke has just said. My stomach lurches like I just swallowed a live frog. I can't tear my eyes away from the blatant flirting even though it causes me physical pain.

I watch the stunning girl effortlessly execute the world's most subtle, elegant seduction. She has assets at her disposal, and she knows exactly how to use them: her bright sparkly teeth flashing a winning smile; her hand grazing his elbow with each of his witty remarks; her practiced posture—boobs forward, one long shapely leg bent like she's posing on the red carpet. If it weren't my boyfriend at stake, I'd actually be impressed, and even take mental notes in the hope that I could one day have the confidence to pull it off. Everything about her and the spectacle of their conversation brings out all of my insecurities. All the worries that once consumed me about dating Luke are again rising to the surface. I am feeling young and inexperienced and supremely unsexy. I wasn't ready to have sex with Luke, but clearly there is no shortage of girls who are. Is he open to this blatant come-on because I am too inexperienced and immature? Does a girl who knows what she's doing look really good to him ever since I put on the brakes in the hot tub?

Marley and Cate, two girls on my relay team, walk over to the bench to grab their bags. Cate turns to see what I'm staring at.

"Who's that?" she asks, obviously referring to the blonde.

"I have no idea," I say.

Marley checks out the girl. "She won the sprint medley."

"I don't think that's the issue," Cate says.

"Oh, right," says Marley. "You and Luke are together, right?"

I don't have an answer.

"Were you guys exclusive?" Cate asks. The past tense of her question feels like a slap.

Chow is in the distance, wrangling the team onto the bus back to school. Cate and Marley walk off, and

I hurry to catch up with them in order to avoid contact with Luke. I am full of fury, embarrassment, and jealousy —three terrible sensations wreaking havoc in my body. I don't want to look at Luke, much less talk to him. I need to calm down and let time pass so I don't sound like a possessive lunatic when I finally confront him. And what do I even have to confront him with? He had a conversation with a pretty girl? He permitted another female, one with splendor oozing out of her pores, to flirt with him? Just thinking about it makes me feel foolish, but I can't help it. He looked at her with those glistening eyes and that warm smile, the same smile that makes me feel special. Now I just feel stupid.

I grab a seat toward the back of the bus with Marley and Cate, who gladly share their Corn Nuts and trail mix with me. Luke boards the bus and takes a glance around. I try not to look at him, but I do catch his eye, and he gives me a confused look as if to ask, *WTF?* I just turn away and grab another handful of trail mix. He sits down at the front and gives me the space he can tell I need.

CHAPTER TWENTY-FIVE

THE NEXT DAY after school there is no track workout, and I meet Brett at Starbucks for coffee and homework. Things have been a little different between Brett and me. He still drives me to school most mornings, and we work well together on debate. But I'm less available on the weekends for movie nights or impromptu frozen yogurt runs. I've missed him, and I think that he misses me, too, but he hasn't given me a hard time about it. There's no doubt in my mind he's got some very strong opinions on the matter. I am grateful that he's kept those thoughts to himself.

When I texted him last night, asking, *HW session tomorrow?* he responded right away with: *Starbucks @ 3:15?*

"Where's the big man?" he wants to know right off the bat.

"I'm not his keeper," I say with an undeniable edge to my voice. I should have just said that I didn't know and that just because I have a boyfriend doesn't mean I can't hang out with my friend. But calling Luke my boyfriend right now feels a little silly and wrong. After the track meet, Luke got off the bus back at school, got right into his Jeep, and left. We didn't text or FaceTime last night. As mad as I was, I was hoping to connect with him and make everything better. But instead, I clung tightly to my silent phone, doing my homework and hoping to hear from him.

"Trouble in paradise?" Brett asks with a smirk.

"Sort of."

I tell Brett the annoying and embarrassing story about the meet and the blonde and my jealousy. I expect him to tell me I'm being paranoid, but instead he says that guys like Luke are weak and if a pretty girl is willing to make herself available, you can't expect him to ignore it. This only deepens my insecurities. As long as I have crushes and boyfriends and relationships, I have a lifetime of jealousy in my future. I put my head on the table in mock drama and Brett pats me on the back.

"Janey, come on, what did you expect to happen?" he asks.

"What do you mean?" I ask.

"I mean, Luke and his friends think they're kings. They're not exactly boyfriend material."

I lift my head off the table and look him in the eye. "You don't know him," I say.

"Do you?" Brett asks, genuinely curious.

"Yes, I do. He's not like that. He loves me," I say.

"Be careful, Janey," Brett says. "I'm sure Luke says everything right to get what he wants."

"That's really not how it is," I say, but I'm starting to question my conviction.

"He's an expert," Brett warns. "Don't be a fool. I don't want to see you get hurt."

"That makes two of us," I say.

"What's going to happen after graduation?" Brett asks.

"He's leaving for Boston," I say. "And never coming back."

"Never?" he asks.

"Well, his parents are moving there and selling their house here. So, yeah, *never* might be kind of accurate," I say.

Brett takes a big gulp of his coffee. "Then you need to be even more careful."

"Why is that?" I ask.

"Because he's not going to do the long-distance-romance thing. He's going to leave for college and leave you behind. Trust me, that kind of player does not wait around for his high school girlfriend."

"How are you so sure?" I ask.

"Because I know guys like that," he says.

It's time to call Brett on his shit. "Brett, you think you know guys like Luke, but aren't they just stereotypes that you've built up in your head? Have you ever really gotten to know a guy like Luke?"

"I don't need to," he says. "And I'm not sure I want to."

"You're one of my best friends, and he's my boyfriend. It would be nice if you gave him a chance," I say.

"I'll give him a chance when I'm sure he's treating you the way you deserve to be treated. And after what happened yesterday, I'm not so sure."

I can't argue with him on that. Damn Brett and his excellent debate skills.

"Well, I think this is my cue to exit," Brett says with his eye on the door. I look up and see Luke and a bunch of other senior guys walk up to the counter. "Keep me posted. If he makes things right, I'll be more open-minded about him. But I need to know that he's worthy of you." Brett puts his backpack over his shoulder and takes his keys out of his pocket. He gives me a hug and leaves.

Luke catches sight of me and stops in his tracks. This time I don't look away. We stare at each other. I am determined to not be the first to break the trance. Maybe he is just as determined as I am, because an uncomfortably long time passes while we stare at each other from opposite corners. Finally, he turns away to place his order.

I am completely out of my element here. Brett's words are sticking to my insides, making me queasy. The picture he painted of Luke is engraved in my brain. Luke is sitting at a table ten feet away, and I'm totally unclear as to our status. Who is supposed to initiate the effort to make things better? I miss my old life—so simple, so free of drama and strategy. I grab my stuff and leave, my head down, trying to move past the senior boys quickly and without being noticed.

I'm walking home feeling more alone than I have felt in a very long time. My whole life is upside down, and I want to cry. I miss Luke but I'm mad at him. I miss my parents living at home together and I'm really mad at them for splitting up.

I'm about two blocks from home when, in my peripheral vision, I see a black Jeep pull up next to me. I don't even have to turn my head to know that it's Luke. I feel both relief and anxiety wash over me like a wave.

"Get in," he says, and I practically jump into his car.

We drive in silence for a minute or two.

"You want to tell me what's up?" he asks. That perpetual Luke Hallstrom grin is conspicuously absent, and his serious demeanor is unfamiliar to me.

I have no idea what to say. I haven't planned for this conversation and I need to buy a little time to contemplate my response. "I don't know," I say.

"You don't know?" he asks, incredulous. "Well, if you don't know, who does? I certainly don't. What happened at that track meet, Janey?"

"I don't know," I repeat, feeling and sounding like a fool.

"Well, something must have happened," he says. "I got on the bus and you didn't even look at me. I've been waiting to hear from you. It's like you flipped a switch. I think I deserve an explanation."

I have no choice but to be honest. "I saw you shamelessly flirting with that girl," I say, and I am well aware of how juvenile I sound.

"What girl?" Luke asks with genuine confusion. I see him wracking his brain in an effort to replay the events of yesterday afternoon. It's incredible that what looked to me like a significant and very memorable conversation where real sexual attraction was brewing seems to have meant absolutely nothing to him.

"The blonde from Escondido."

"Oh. Her? She's a friend of Amanda's. Really? You iced me because you saw me talking to her? That's a little crazy, isn't it?"

"She seemed so into you. And you looked very happy about it. I felt jealous and I didn't know how to deal with it. I panicked."

Luke takes a big breath. "I'm sorry you felt bad, but you can't just go silent without telling me what's going on."

"I realize that," I say.

"You're my girlfriend. I told you I love you." He says it as though carrying that around is supposed to make me impervious to worry and skepticism.

"I know," I say.

"But . . ." he trails off.

"But what?" I need to know what is on the other side of that sentence. Fear rises from my stomach straight through to my heart.

"But the jealous-girlfriend thing doesn't really work for me," he says. My first instinct is to just apologize and beg for forgiveness, but I know I would hate myself later.

"I'm sorry I have feelings that don't *work for you*," I say, and I hear the edge creeping into my voice, "but they are real and I'm sharing them with you."

"Well, I don't really know what to do with that," he says. He looks at me and I can't tell what he's feeling. I search for the warmth I always see sparkling in his eyes. He seems different, like he's really confused and unsure where to go from here. He pulls up in front of my house and turns off the engine. He turns to me, his face grim.

"Would you rather I didn't tell you how I was feeling?" I ask.

"I'm just surprised you're so insecure." His words cut to my core, making me feel more insecure than ever. I will myself to stay strong and not crumble under his intense scrutiny.

"Again, I can't help the way I feel, and I thought I could talk to you about it," I say, hoping I sound much braver than I feel.

"Well, that's the thing, Janey. You *didn't* talk to me about it. You just assumed the worst. I had to pick you up on the side of the road to find out what was going on. I deserve better than that." He's right.

"You're right," I say.

"It doesn't seem like you trust me," he says.

"I do," I say.

"Doesn't seem like it," he says, looking right at me, his eyes sad. "I can't be with someone who doesn't trust me." There's a finality in his voice that scares the hell out of me.

I am stunned into silence. We sit there in the quiet for what feels like hours, but it is probably less than a minute.

"I want my girlfriend to trust me. Do you know what you want?" he asks.

I know what I *don't* want. I don't want to feel the way I feel now. I don't want self-doubt to make me jealous and dramatic. Before I have a chance to answer, Luke speaks up.

"Maybe you need some space. A little time to think about what you want," he says gravely.

Those are the scariest words I've heard since my parents told me they were separating. There's nothing to think about. I want Luke. I love him. Loving him as much as I do is why I felt insecure. Isn't that obvious? If I didn't care so much about him, I wouldn't mind if he flirted with every girl in San Diego County.

But I don't say those things. Instead I just say "Okay." I reach for the door handle, hoping he'll make me stay in his car until we turn this around and get back to the fun and the kissing. I want to see his face break into that smile that turns me to butter. But there's no smile, no sign of his adorable tongue. What do I do? What do I say? Is this over?

I take hold of my backpack, swing the door open, and get out of the Jeep. I stand there on the curb, looking at him.

"Bye, Janey," he says.

"Bye," I say, closing the door and walking slowly into my house.

CHAPTER TWENTY-SIX

I WALK INTO MY HOUSE, drop my stuff on the floor, and start to cry. Even though I'm sad about my parents splitting up and I miss my dad and I'm stressed about all the changes in my life, these tears are for Luke. I don't want to lose him.

I handled this situation badly. I behaved like a jealous little girl. But is he blameless? What about the fact that he's a giant flirt? Am I just supposed to be okay watching girls fall all over him?

Within the hour, Sloan and Danielle are at my house for some much-needed counseling. They came as soon as I texted, but not before stopping at 7-Eleven to grab bags of Hot Tamales and Pretzel M&M's. We sit on my bed discussing every word that was exchanged between Luke and me. We analyze his dating past, his so-called *friendships* with every girl we know, and his penchant for flirting. We stalk his social media. There is no shortage of photos of him with a wide variety of girls.

"Maybe Brett is right about Luke," I say.

"Brett is a cynical virgin," Sloan says. We look at Sloan and smile at her word choice. "I, on the other hand, am a wise, experienced virgin," she adds. "Two very different things."

"Luke's not a player; he's just a flirt," Danielle adds.

"Remind me of the difference," I say.

Sloan says, "A player hooks up a lot and never has a girlfriend. A flirt makes girls feel like he wants to hook up with them, but at the end of the day, he doesn't really do anything."

"So you're saying he wants everyone to like him," I say.

"Basically," Sloan admits while she sifts through the M&M's, pulling out all the blue ones.

"Is that true?" I ask. "Does Luke want everyone to like him?"

"Doesn't everyone?" Danielle asks, playing devil's advocate.

"You know what I mean," I say. "Does he thrive on knowing that every girl wants him?"

"That's probably accurate," Danielle says.

"You know," I say, "he is still close with Amanda and Julia. Most people have nothing to do with their exes."

"Yeah," says Sloan, "he probably hopes they're still in love with him."

"And they probably are," I say.

"Of course they are—he's Luke Hallstrom," Sloan says, popping a Hot Tamale into her mouth.

"Well, I think we've determined one thing here," Danielle says.

"What's that?" I ask.

"Perfect Luke Hallstrom actually has a flaw. He's a people-pleaser who feels the need to ensure every girl he meets falls madly in love with him and stays that way."

"Ugh! What am I supposed to do?"

Danielle says, "You have to decide if that's the person you want to be with."

"Remember," Sloan warns, "he's not going to change."

"Who are we kidding? It might not be up to me to decide. He thinks I'm young and insecure and that I don't trust him," I say. "This might already be over."

"If you want him, you'll have to convince him otherwise," Danielle says.

I get up from the bed and go over to my closet and take out the bracelet Luke got me for Valentine's Day. I took it off for the track meet and didn't put it back on because I have been feeling so unsure about where Luke and I stand. The card is folded into a tiny square and jammed into the narrow black box. I read the card for the hundredth time. *Love, Luke.* I wrap the bracelet around my wrist and fasten the tiny clasp.

"I want him," I say.

CHAPTER TWENTY-SEVEN

AT 9:30 THAT NIGHT, I find myself parked in my mom's car in front of Luke's house. During dinner at home, my mom must have asked me ten times if everything was okay, and I came up with an equal number of excuses for why I was so distracted and quiet. The last thing I needed was my mother to confirm Luke's theory that I'm not ready for a relationship.

After Danielle and Sloan left, I tried desperately to do my homework, with zero success. The only thing on my mind was Luke. I love him. I'm not ready to let him walk away because he's popular and is always going to have girls surrounding him. He's a flirt, and that's not going to change. I have to deal with the fact that there's something about Luke that I don't like. I've got to gain the strength to accept him as he is. The realization that I don't think he's absolutely perfect is actually somewhat liberating. He's human. It kind of makes him even easier to love. The big question is, does he still think I'm lovable? Am I on the list of people whose affection he wants to maintain?

I can't seem to get out of the car. It's cold outside, and even though I have the engine running and the heat blasting, I'm still shivering. Raindrops start falling on the windshield. I did not bring a raincoat or an umbrella. I could use the rain as an excuse to blow off this ill-advised plan and just drive home. I look out the windshield and up at his house. His Jeep is parked in the driveway, and lights glow through the upstairs windows.

I have to psych myself up to walk to the front door and ring the bell. The rain is quickening, beating on the roof of the car. I remind myself about the final piece of advice Danielle offered: *Do not leave there until you've said what you need to say.* Danielle and Sloan prepped me with words and phrases to use, but I can't seem to recall a single one of them. I'm going to have to wing it.

I turn off the engine, which makes the pounding of the rain seem even louder. I dash from the car to the covered porch, but not before my hair and clothes get supremely soaked. Before I totally chicken out, I ring the bell. After an almost insufferable moment, I hear footsteps. Mrs. Hallstrom opens the door.

"Hi, Mrs. Hallstrom," I say, as if my standing in front of her house in the pouring rain is a regular occurrence.

"Hi, Janey. You're dripping. Come in." I step inside the house, careful to not stand on her Persian foyer rug in my wet Converse. "Is Luke expecting you?"

Just as I'm about to answer, I look up to find Luke standing at the top of the stairs.

"Hi," he says as he descends toward me. His mom makes a prompt exit to the kitchen. "What are you doing here?" he asks. Now, there's a loaded question. *I'm here to beg you to take me back? I came to tell you that I might be insecure, but you've got issues too?* Where are all those carefully rehearsed words I practiced with Sloan and Danielle?

"I want to talk," I said.

"Come on up," he says.

I leave my soggy sneakers in a corner by the front door and follow Luke up the stairs. We walk down a long hallway and enter his bedroom. He closes the door. His room looks like the work of a decorator. It is done in navy and gray, with roman shades that coordinate with an upholstered headboard and duvet cover. The mahogany bookshelves match the wood of the crown molding. Despite the professional touches, the room is all Luke. His trophies are everywhere, from the shelves to his desk and even on the floor. There are two U2 posters on the wall alongside a framed Boston Red Sox signed jersey. Luke moves his computer, iPad, and school binders off of his bed to free up some space for me.

"Have a seat," he says. His tone is significantly friendlier than it was in the car, but there is still a palpable distance between us.

"Thanks," I say, trying to figure out how to sit on a

boy's bed. He leans against the headboard, and I sit near the foot of the bed on a navy blue throw blanket.

"What did you want to talk about?" He seems genuinely interested.

"I've been giving a lot of thought to the conversation we had in your car," I say, fidgeting with the fringe on the blanket.

"And?" he says, lifting his eyebrows in curiosity.

"And I know that I overreacted. I was jealous. I never felt that way before, and I didn't know what to do. I'm sorry."

"Okay," he says. "That's fair, I guess."

"I've been one hundred percent honest with you about that fact that this is all new for me. Sometimes you're going to see signs of my inexperience."

"Janey, it's fine to be inexperienced. It's not fine to assume the worst. Especially when I've done nothing to show I can't be trusted."

"You're right. You deserve the benefit of the doubt."

"Why is there even a doubt?" he asks now, a slight smile creeping onto his lips. Do I dare say it?

"Well . . ." I say, hesitant to call him out.

"Well what?" The mood in the room is lightening, his smile threatening to make an appearance.

"You're a big flirt," I say. He takes a moment to digest this. He seems surprised, which is sort of shocking to me. Is this really breaking news?

"I am not," he argues, a hint of teasing in his voice.

"Oh yes you are. Admit it," I say, trying to echo his tone.

"I'm with you. I love you. But I also happen to be a nice guy, so I'm going to be friendly to people. You're still the one I want."

"I know."

"You know what?"

"That you're a nice guy."

"What about the other parts?" he asks.

"What do you mean?" I ask, looking down at the blue blanket fringe tangled up in my fingers.

"Do you also know that I love you and that you're the one I want?"

"Yes," I say.

"Say it," he says.

"You love me and I'm the one you want."

"You know, when I see you at track, or with your friends, it's obvious that you know exactly who you are. There's nothing fake about you. I love that you're so confident."

I can't believe that he thinks I'm confident, when I usually feel exactly the opposite. If he only knew that he is the one who makes me feel beautiful in a way I never allowed myself to feel. Because of Luke, I can stand naked in front of a mirror and appreciate my body. Shockingly, I can stand naked in front of him and accept his appreciation of my body. I never would have thought that possible. It's all because of Luke.

"Well, I guess we've debunked that theory, haven't we?" I say.

"No. You had a moment of weakness. But you've gotta talk to me when you're pissed. Don't freeze me out."

"Got it."

"Come here," he says as he leans toward me. I drop the blanket and crawl up toward him. We kiss hungrily. We go from zero to sixty in about half a second, and the kissing is suddenly crazy hot. It's as though all the feelings I've had in the last twenty-four hours—jealousy, fear, insecurity, anger, relief, and happiness—are in a blender, being whipped up into a frenzy and working themselves out of me via the most intense make-out session ever. He pulls me onto his lap and I straddle him. He leans back against his pile of blue and gray pillows and I lean forward against him.

His hands reach down my pants and grab my ass. Feeling his strong hands on my butt makes me even hotter for him. I hear myself moan and quickly realize we are in his house and his mom is downstairs.

"What about your parents?" I ask.

"Don't worry about them," he answers, unwilling to let his mouth separate from mine.

I push myself down on him so my legs press tighter around his, and his crotch pushes up against mine. We find a rhythm—kissing, pressing, pushing, moaning, grabbing. Just as I think I'm going to explode, the home phone rings and we hear his dad's voice from down the hall. The trance is broken. We come apart and look at each other. We're both flushed and a little sweaty. I stare at him and I know. I know at some point in the very near future I'm going to lose my virginity to Luke Hallstrom.

CHAPTER TWENTY-EIGHT

SATURDAY, DANIELLE, SLOAN, AND I go shopping and out to lunch. It's the kind of beautiful San Diego day that we refer to as a sweaters-and-sunglasses day. After lunch at The Promiscuous Fork, we walk around La Jolla, poking into shops. In one store, I come across a beautiful white lace nightgown. It's short and has spaghetti straps and is practically see through. It's somehow both naughty and nice. I take it into the fitting room to try it on. Even as I take off my leggings and sweatshirt, before I even have the nightgown off the hanger, I wonder how and when I would wear it. I slip the nightgown over my head and stare at my reflection.

There I am. Janey King. Wearing lingerie, of all things. It looks kinda pretty. Maybe even a little sexy. Wow! That's a new thing for me. I actually think those very words when looking at my own reflection. I like how my chest and arms look. I appreciate my muscular legs, and even my small boobs look cute and perky under the delicate fabric. I picture Luke lying on a bed and me walking into the room wearing this nightgown. I don't know if it will work that way, but it can't hurt to have a plan. I look at the price tag. It's been reduced from a hundred and fifty dollars to seventy-five. Yikes. Seventy-five bucks is still steep. I decide to wait and give it some thought.

"Not good?" Sloan wants to know as I replace the hanger on the rack.

"It's gorgeous," I say. "Just a little out of my price range. Probably not that practical anyway."

"Practical, schmatical," Sloan says. "We're talking about your first time. It should be special, and you should feel special."

"Maybe," I say. "I'll think about it."

The three of us continue down the street. More shopping, more talking. We take a break at Rocky Mountain Chocolate Factory. We sit at a small table outside with one Oreo-crusted caramel apple to share among us. Sloan tells us all about Ryan Webb, the sophomore she's been hanging out with. She's had her eye on him since he started as a freshman and we were sophomores.

"Is this your first younger guy?" I ask.

"Yup," she responds. "And it's so fun being the older woman. I get to teach him. We haven't done much, and that part is fun too. Nice to take it slow."

"Speaking of taking it slow"—Danielle turns to me— "you seem to be getting ready."

"Oh?" I say. "How do you figure?"

"If you're trying on sexy lingerie, you're definitely thinking about having sex," Sloan says.

"It's true," I confess. "I think I'm ready."

"You're smart," Danielle says. "I wish I had waited until I knew for sure I was ready. I thought it was time and I was supposed to do it, so I just figured I'd get used to it. And yeah, now I'm used to it and I love Charlie, but I felt so uneasy and insecure the night I lost my virginity. That won't happen for you and Luke. It will be beautiful."

"I hope so," I say nervously.

"We know *you'll* be beautiful," Sloan says. She gives Danielle a knowing look and reaches into one of her shopping bags.

"Surprise!" Danielle chirps as Sloan pulls out the white nightgown I tried on.

I'm stunned. "You guys! That's crazy! What did you do?"

"What are friends for?" Sloan says.

"How did you do this?" I ask.

"Remember when I said I left my phone in the dressing room?" Sloan asks. I nod, putting the pieces together. "I went back and picked it up for you. It's an early birthday present from both of us."

"Now when Luke peels it off you, you'll think of us," Danielle says.

"Awesome. I'll be naked with him, thinking of you. What's wrong with that picture?" We all laugh hysterically. Thank god for best friends.

CHAPTER TWENTY-NINE

*I*T'S OUR FIRST regular season track meet. I'm in the locker room getting pumped. Cate is blasting "Walk This Way" by Run-D.M.C. and all the track girls are singing and dancing while they secure their ponytails and double-knot their running shoes. I tuck my La Jolla High Track tank top into my shorts and walk out the door with a bunch of other girls. As I make my way to the track, I see that the stands are full. Parents and students from both schools have come to root for their kids and their friends. I'm sure my mom and dad are somewhere out there, but I can't see them in the crowd. I do see Brett, sitting in the front row. We catch each other's eye and he gives me a thumbs-up.

Before my feet even hit the all-weather surface of the track, I feel a strong arm around my shoulders. Luke whispers in my ear, "Go get 'em, Peachy Keen." He looks so hot in his track uniform, his biceps defined, his legs long and powerful. We walk to the center of the field together, his arm never moving from its perch on my shoulder.

I look up into the stands, feeling slightly self-conscious knowing that my parents can see me standing on the grass with a guy's arm around me. A guy who is a virtual stranger to them.

I scan each row of bleachers, and I finally see my mom's floppy hat. She bought it when we first arrived in Cabo and wore it every day of the trip. That thing was everywhere: on the beach, by the pool . . . it even fell off a boat into the ocean. My dad, ever the hero, jumped off the boat to rescue my mother's nineteen-dollar hat. Just seeing the faded pink in a sea of school-spirit colors sends an unexpected pang through my heart.

Suddenly, it hits me that Cabo was the last vacation we will ever have as a family. I was so clueless while we basked in the sun and drank virgin strawberry margaritas, entirely unaware of the news I would receive on New Year's Eve. Even though it was relatively recent, everything was different about my life when my mom wore that hat. I had never kissed Luke. I had never had my skin tingle at the touch of his hand. I had never seen him naked. I had never purchased condoms. I had never thought of myself as beautiful. I had never thought that my family would break apart.

My mom sees that I have caught sight of her and she gives the smallest of waves, really just a slight movement of two fingers. I wave back even smaller, merely raising my hand to acknowledge her presence. My body feels like it's sinking into the freshly mown grass of the field.

"You okay?" Luke asks, removing his arm from around my shoulders and facing me.

"Yeah," I say, exhaling deeply as though to expel from my body and mind the medley of sadness, longing, and realization. "I'm going to get some water." I walk over to the giant Gatorade tanks that are lined up near the benches and pour myself some ice-cold water. I've got to shake off the sadness, get my head on straight, and get ready to run my ass off.

The various track team groups begin to gather in their respective areas. I'm so glad that the 300-meter low hurdles are first. I have stiff competition in a senior from Point Loma. As soon as I hear the gun, I get off to a good start. My dad, who ran track in college, always made me skip to build leg strength and refine my technique. He and I would go out to the track on the weekends and, together, we would skip fifty meters with our knees as high as possible. Then we would rest for one minute and repeat. After ten of these, we were both exhausted and ready for milkshakes.

As I clear each hurdle, I am careful to look ahead to the next one as opposed to down at my knee, which is a mistake I used to make. In my peripheral vision, I see Point Loma at my side. I run faster. She does, too. As I push to regain the lead, I hear a crash—she has kicked over a hurdle. I finish strong and take the blue ribbon. I look to the stands to see my parents cheering with enthusiasm. Luke, from the long jump area, gives me a congratulatory nod. I feel invincible.

I have a slight break before the 4x800 meter relay. I'm the anchor, the last leg, which I love because if we're behind, I know how to catch up. Cate leads us off. After the first hundred meters, she cuts to the post and takes the lead. Senior Lindsay Caines is our second runner. Lindsay establishes her position in the exchange zone and makes eye contact with Cate as she approaches with the baton. Lindsay is careful not to take off too fast, because she can tell that Cate is fading. They get their steps in line and Lindsay gets the stick. Lindsay keeps us in first place, keeping a safe distance ahead of the competition. She runs her two laps with ease, closing in on Marley, our third runner. Marley, her receiving hand up, yells for the stick.

The key to a good exchange is the arm and hand coordination of both runners. Marley gets the baton and takes off at a good pace. She maintains the lead and approaches me to pass the stick for the final leg. We execute a blind hand-off as I grasp the baton with my right hand and pull it from Marley, who is holding it loosely in her left hand, making the transfer as smooth as silk. I run, and without looking behind me, I get the sense that I am increasing the distance between myself and the other teams, as the sound of their footsteps grows fainter. Before I know it, the finish line is within inches and I cross it, never letting up. My teammates join me and we jump up and down in celebration of our first victory of the season.

At the end of the meet, La Jolla High has the most ribbons. Luke takes first place in long jump as well as the high jump, and he comes in second place in the triple jump, an event he hates but Chow makes him do. Parents and friends from the stands are now gathering on the track, seeking out the people they came to watch. I see my parents approaching from one direction and Luke making his way across the field from another. Here we go. My mom and dad get to me first.

"Congrats, babe!" my dad says, giving me a hug. He doesn't care that I'm sweaty and my uniform is sticking to me. "You looked fantastic out there."

"Thanks, Daddy."

"That was fabulous," Mom chimes in.

"Thank you, Mom," I say, and I lean into her while she kisses my forehead. "We watched Luke, too; he was terrific."

My mom's words are still lingering in the air as Luke approaches. I'm almost positive he heard his name, making me cringe with embarrassment. Why do parents always have the wrong thing to say at exactly the wrong time? Luke, ever the gentleman, pretends he doesn't know my mom was talking about him.

"Hi," he says.

"Nice to see you, Luke." Dad puts out his hand and Luke partakes in a manly handshake.

"Mr. King," Luke says, "how are you?"

"Please, call me Robert, and this is Karen," Dad says, welcoming Mom to the conversation.

"Great to finally meet you, Luke," my mom says. *Finally?* Why did she have to say *finally?* Now Luke might think I've been talking to my parents about him for eons. Okay, I'm overthinking again. Standing here with my parents and Luke has me totally on edge. I need to take a deep breath and chill.

Luke doesn't seem to notice the details that make me wince. "Nice to meet you, too," Luke says. "How'd you like the meet? Your daughter was awesome, wasn't she?"

Mom and Dad chime in with their biased praise of my performance. Luke eagerly agrees. Then Mom tells Luke how well he did. I am back to overthinking. I worry that it seems like she watched him too carefully. Does he think my creepy mom was stalking him at his track meet? I know I'm being extra sensitive and super paranoid, but I can't help it. Every word, every sound my parents utter is subject to my intense scrutiny and criticism. I am looking at them through what I imagine to be Luke's perspective. I want them to say and do everything right.

Chow calls Luke over to help take the mats into the shed and Luke expertly extricates himself from the conversation with my mom and dad.

"I've gotta go help clean up. See you soon, I hope," he says and dashes away to fulfill his duties as captain of the track team.

Mom and Dad, predictably, gush about how nice, polite, handsome, and mature Luke is. I love hearing it. I could stand there for hours and listen to them spout off about the many wonderful attributes of my boyfriend. And they don't even know the best parts—how he kisses, how his sweet tongue sticks out when he laughs, how he makes me feel like the most beautiful girl in the world.

"I'm going to run some errands before I head home. Need anything?" Mom asks.

"No, I'm good," I say. She gives me a kiss on the cheek and then says goodbye to my dad, and he gets a similar peck on the cheek. Very polite, like a kiss she would give a friend of the family. I come to the realization that I've never seen my parents kiss each other on the cheek. It's not like they showed a lot of PDA or made out in front of me or anything, but whenever they parted or reunited it was always with a kiss on the lips. Those kisses on the lips are now a thing of the past. I find that these little reminders of how things have changed are constantly taking me by surprise and tugging at my heart.

After Mom has gone, Dad reaches into his pocket. "I have something for you," he says. He produces a small wire ring holding two keys. "This one is for the building," he says, fingering the brass key, "and this one is for my apartment." He shows me the silver key.

"Oh. Thanks," I say.

"You live there, too, and you can go there whenever

you feel like it," he says. "I have a trip this weekend, so you can hang out there if you want. Don't sleep there when I'm gone, and make sure your mom knows where you are. But treat it like home. It's stocked with Frosted Flakes and string cheese."

"Thanks, Dad."

"Have fun." My dad's timing is eerie. There's no hint of knowing to his tone or his expression. He doesn't nod toward Luke, or wink, or do anything disgusting. He's simply straightforward and generous, as though he just wants me to be comfortable sharing his new life. I grasp the ring in my hand, feeling the cool metal of the keys, and I feel like everything is falling into place. I'm going to lose my virginity this weekend.

That night, I'm sitting on my bed studying for an American history test when I hear the faintest of knocks on my bedroom door. I turn down my music.

"Come in," I call. My mom walks in timidly.

"Hi," she says. "You busy?"

"Big history test tomorrow on World War II," I say.

"I'm sure you'll do great," she says. "Can we talk for a minute?"

"Sure." Uh-oh. I brace myself for what's going to come next. She sits on the edge of my bed, moving my laptop and history book to my nightstand. I cautiously await the inquisition.

"Luke seems great," she says.

"Yeah, he is," I say with a tight smile, anticipating the onslaught of questions.

"How serious is it?" she wants to know.

"I don't know. I like him, he likes me, but we're not getting married anytime soon, if that's what you're asking." I know damn well that's not what she's asking. She knows damn well that I know that's not what she's asking.

"Do you love him?"

Yes! I love him like crazy! I think of him constantly and am strongly considering having sex with him this weekend in Dad's peaceful apartment by the beach.

"Maybe." Why am I unwilling to open up to her about this? I've always shared everything with my mom. She's easygoing and trusting. She always offers excellent advice. She's sweet and smart and has never been judgmental or steered me wrong. And yet, I feel dead-set on keeping my Luke story a secret from her . . . for now.

"It's easy to see that he loves you, too," she says. "Remember I only want the best for you. And I love you more than you can imagine." She strokes my hair.

"Thanks, Mommy," I say, my heart melting a bit for a woman whose life is changing just as quickly as mine is.

"And I'm here for you. Whatever you might need. If you ever want to talk, I'm here to listen."

"I love you so much," I say, and I lean into her and welcome her arms around me. I inhale her familiar smell—a mix of perfume and cocoa-butter hand lotion—a smell that, since I was a little girl, has always made me feel safe and at peace. I'm lucky that she cares and that she supports me, and it still feels good to have my mom on my bed next to me, holding me tight. But I also need my independence. Who knows, maybe all those self-possessed girls I notice at track meets, in locker rooms, and at debate tournaments also sometimes still need their mommies.

CHAPTER THIRTY

O N FRIDAY MORNING I wake up at 6:28 a.m.,
two minutes before my alarm is set to go off. I
have two minutes to lie in bed. Two minutes to
think. I don't have to think. I know. I'm ready.

Part of my morning ritual is packing my bag for
track practice. Running shoes, shorts, jog bra, socks, T-
shirt, sweatshirt. This morning I add the white nightgown
Sloan and Danielle bought for me. It's still carefully folded
in tissue, deep inside the store's pink paper bag. Since I
brought it home, I have not even opened the bag. I was
afraid to get it dirty or misplace the receipt in case I decided to return it. I thought that trying it on or putting it
in my underwear or pajama drawer would somehow jinx
everything.

I dig deep into my bathing-suit drawer to fish out
the condoms. How many should I bring? One seems
foolish—I've heard they can break. Ten is probably too
many—I don't want to set unrealistic expectations. Five

has got to be about right. Five it is. An assortment of the different kinds, so Luke can choose.

Where is the appropriate place to carry condoms? After much consideration, and a few bad ideas poorly executed, I wrap the five condoms into the crinkly tissue next to the soft white nightgown inside the pink bag. Then I put the pink bag in the bottom of my track duffle, underneath the worn shoes, the yellowed socks, and the gray sweatshirt with the frayed cuffs. Then I grab the keys my dad gave me and tuck them into the side zippered pocket inside the Nike bag.

I hear Brett honking for me in my driveway. Brett has tried hard to be a supportive friend, even though I can tell it kills him a little to pretend he thinks Luke is good for me. One morning, as Brett and I were walking to class from the parking lot, Luke came up from behind us and grabbed my hand and held it as the three of us walked together.

"What's up, man?" Luke asked Brett, friendly as ever.

"Not much," Brett answered, visibly unsure of how to talk to Luke. I sensed Brett's discomfort, but just before I chimed in to ease the tension, Brett beat me to it.

"Did you watch the Celtics collapse last night?"

"Yes!" Luke said enthusiastically. "I can't believe we lost to the freakin' Trailblazers."

"In double OT," Brett adds.

"Awful. We would have had that game if we made our free throws."

"That's a bad loss," Brett said like it pained him.

I know Brett well enough to say with absolute certainty that he did not watch that game. I also happen to know that he scours news sites in the morning so he's always up to speed on all current events—even the NBA, which is of little interest to him. He made an effort to talk to my boyfriend, and I love him for it.

Now I grab all my stuff and run out the door. I smile at the odd assortment of items I'm secretly toting. I can't help but think of the worst that could happen: What if the seam of the bag rips, spilling the entire contents in the school hallway for all to see? What if I have the same Nike duffle bag as someone else in the locker room, and that someone else opens it, only to find evidence of my romantic plans?

At track practice, I can't stop staring at Luke. He seems to notice that every time he turns around, I'm looking at him. He stares back, as if to say, *What's up with you today, girl?* The grueling hour-and-a-half practice takes forever to come to its eventual end. Every stretch, every drill, every sprint seems to be happening in agonizing slow motion. At long last, Chow blows his whistle and says, "Good workout."

Luke approaches me as I grab some water from the Gatorade vat. "Chow was insane today," he says, out of breath.

"I'm in the mood to go for a little run off campus, how about you?" I say.

"Are you nuts?" he asks. "I'm totally wiped out."

"You're kind of a lightweight, aren't you?" I tease.

"I can't believe you haven't had enough," he says, incredulous.

"I can't believe you poop out so easily," I say, challenging him. I start to jog away, and after a few steps, I turn around and jog backward, looking at him. "What's it gonna be, Mr. Track Scholarship? A few extra miles more than you can stand? Maybe that's something the Boston College coach should know." I keep jogging backward, looking at Luke until he finally gives in, throws his cup in the trash, and runs after me. I turn around and run forward, jogging off the school grounds and into the surrounding neighborhood.

Luke is now at my side and we run together in a nice easy lope along the suburban streets near La Jolla High. The driveways of the single-story family homes are littered with kids who are visibly joyful that it's Friday afternoon. Some walk home from school with friends, backpacks light for the weekend. Others ride their skateboards or write on the sidewalk with thick pieces of pastel-colored chalk.

"You're funny today," Luke says.

"How so?" I know damn well how so, but I'm curious what he'll say.

"I'm not sure, but something is different. Like you have something on your mind."

"I do," I admit. We turn a corner and end up on the La Jolla bike path.

"Want to share?" he asks. "Or do I have to figure it out on my own?"

"I can tell you, but I'm pretty sure you can figure it out." I'm getting nervous. In all my calculations and planning, I never realized I'd have to say the words *I want to have sex with you. Today.*

"Go ahead and tell me. I can be pretty dense."

"Okay," I say and take a deep breath.

"Okay?" he asks with curiosity.

Here goes. Wow. You'd think telling a boy you're ready to sleep with him would be easy. I mean, what guy doesn't want to hear that, right? But it's really scary. Because once I say it, I've made the commitment to do it and, even though I feel certain about my readiness to do it, it's always nice to have the option of chickening out. Another deep breath.

"Will you have sex with me? Today?" There. I did it.

Luke runs right off the path onto the adjacent grass and does a dramatic tumble, ending up lying on his back, hands over his heart. I stop running, walk over to where he lies, and stand over him.

"You all right?" I ask.

He grabs my hand and pulls me onto him. Now I am lying on top of him, in the grass in broad daylight, his arms wrapped tightly around me. My face hovers over his face, our noses almost touching.

"I would love to make love to you," he says.

"Good. Because I've given it a lot of thought, and I'm ready," I say.

"You're absolutely sure?" he asks.

"I'm absolutely sure," I confirm. "Although . . ."

"What?" he asks with concern.

"Please don't say *make love*," I say with a little cringe.

"Too mushy?" he asks.

"It just kinda creeps me out," I say.

He laughs that adorable laugh with his tongue ever so slightly sticking out. "Guess what?"

"What?" I ask.

"I'm going to make love to you." He smiles.

"Fine," I say. "Make sweet love to me, Luke Hallstrom."

We run back to school, and for a guy who was thoroughly exhausted ten minutes ago, he has sure found some energy. I've never seen Luke run so fast. At school, we gather our things and then meet back at his Jeep.

"Any suggestions of a location?" Luke asks.

I pull out the keys to my dad's place. "Head north on La Jolla Boulevard toward Torrey Pines," I say. I've never been so nervous in my life. Every step with Luke brings a new height of nerves. Before our smoothie date, I would have said that I had experienced nervousness in anticipation of a debate or a track meet or a big test. However, now I know what real nerves feel like: heart beating out of my chest, stomach flipping in somersaults, and thoughts racing.

I give Luke directions to my dad's place, but all I can think of is that I can't believe I'm about to have sex. I can't believe Luke is going to be inside me. Will it hurt as much as Danielle said it would? Will I do it right? If I change my mind, will he hate me? Are blue balls a real thing?

"I need to stop," Luke says.

I'm not sure I heard him correctly because the thoughts in my head are so loud.

"What?" I ask.

"I need to make a quick stop to pick something up." It takes me a minute, but then I figure out that he's probably talking about condoms.

"I've got them," I say.

"You do?" he asks.

I reach into my bag and feel around in the tissue to dig out a couple of the condoms. "Are these fine?"

He takes a look at the foil-wrapped rubbers in my hand. "Wow. Yeah. Those will work." He sort of chuckles and shakes his head.

"What?" I ask, wondering if I've done something wrong.

"When you say you're ready, you really mean it," he says.

"Is that good?"

"Are you kidding?" he asks. "It's great. It's a first for me."

"It is?"

"Yeah. Very cool, Janey." For some reason, I am elated

by this revelation. Everything with Luke—the physical as well as the emotional stuff—has been new for me, but not for him. He, the seasoned veteran, has guided me with his expertise. I have just provided a first for him. I am the first girl to bring condoms to the party. Note to self: Be sure to thank Danielle for the excellent advice.

We stop at a red light, and Luke leans over the gearshift to kiss me. I kiss him back with all the excitement and heat that have riddled my body all day long. The driver behind us honks, letting us know the light has turned green. Luke holds tightly to my hand for the rest of the drive.

We park outside and walk through the lobby of my dad's building. As soon as the elevator doors close, we start to kiss. I back up against the wall of the elevator as our hands and tongues explore with a newfound fervor. The heat that always exists when we make out is intensified considerably by all the anticipation.

We enter my dad's apartment and are welcomed by the afternoon sun lighting up the living room. The blue-green of the Pacific Ocean sparkles in the distance.

"Cool place," Luke says.

"Yeah," I agree. I almost add something about how I wish Dad still lived at home with us, but there's no reason to put a damper on the afternoon. We drop our bags on the living room floor.

Luke approaches me, this time with caution and tenderness as opposed to the hot urgency we experienced in the car and in the elevator. He faces me, taking both of my hands in his. He kisses me softly on the lips.

"Hi," he says, almost a whisper.

"Hi," I whisper back.

"I love you." He's still whispering.

"I love you too," I say, echoing his tone.

He takes hold of my sweatshirt and lifts it over my head.

"I think I need to shower first," I say.

"Can I join you?" he asks.

"Sure," I say.

He follows me into my small bathroom. I turn on the shower and the steam from the hot water begins to fill the room. The new white towels hang on the towel rack. Suave shampoo and Dove body soap are the only items on the shower shelf.

I take off my sweaty shirt and jog bra, and he removes his shirt. He reaches for the waistband of my shorts and slides them, along with my underpants, over my hips and onto the floor. I let him look at me, stark naked, allowing myself to be admired and wanted. His shorts fall to the bath mat and his impressive erection stands at full attention. I put my hands on him, feeling his hardness, knowing that it will soon be inside me. I slowly move my hands back and forth, more so to feel him than to please him.

We step into the shower and the hot water bounces between our naked bodies. I stand under the spigot facing Luke, letting my hair and face get drenched. Luke picks up the body soap and squeezes an ample amount into his hands. He moves his soapy hands around my entire body: across my shoulders, over my breasts, around my stomach, and down each arm. He then kneels down to wash my legs, his face right at my crotch. I'm still standing under the beating hot water while he lathers me up, inside and out. It's by far the best feeling I've ever experienced. I feel swollen and tingly throughout my entire body. I look down at him and watch how he watches me, his eyes moving from the work he's doing down there to my face, gauging my reaction.

I gently pull him to standing and take the soap from him to return the favor. I pour the milky white liquid soap directly on his chest and then move my hands across his body, covering every inch with the fresh-smelling foam. His shoulders and chest feel strong under my palms. He turns around and I work on his back and let my hands drift to his butt. I rub his ass and the sides of his legs and then, working up the courage, reach around to the front. I move slowly, gently touching and teasing without intense stroking, keeping in mind that I don't want him to get too close yet.

He turns around, bringing his lathered-up body next to mine under the stream of hot water. His lips on my lips, his chest on my chest, and his penis up against me.

"Wanna take this into the other room?" he whispers into my mouth.

"Yeah," I say.

The soap travels down our bodies and circles the drain. I turn off the water and reach for two towels, handing one to Luke and wrapping one under my arms and around my chest. I step out of the shower and Luke, towel around his waist, follows me into the living room.

The sun is now hanging lower in the sky, giving the whole room an orange hue.

"I'll be right back," I say, and I grab my bag and go into my bedroom. I remove the beautiful nightgown, rip off the tags, and slide it over my head. The smooth fabric feels cool and fresh on my newly washed skin. I take a look in the mirror, and I have to admit, I'm fairly satisfied with how I look. The soft white silk dips down between my breasts, revealing what little cleavage I actually have, and the little flouncy skirt ends at the very tops of my thighs. I shake out my wet hair and take a step out of the bedroom before I remember that the condoms are still in the bag. What am I supposed to do with them? How does one make an entrance with a handful of condoms and still look totally alluring? Not sure it's possible. The truth is, though, there's no way around it. I grab a couple and hide them discreetly behind my back.

"Wow," Luke says. "You look so sexy."

"Thanks," I say, hoping he doesn't notice me tucking the condoms behind a cushion as I pass the sofa. I take the thick brown blanket from the arm of the club chair and spread it on the rug. We sit on the blanket, facing the slid–

ing glass doors and the view of the ocean. Luke's fingers investigate the edge of my nightgown.

"This is really pretty."

"I'm glad you like it," I say.

"Is it new?" he asks.

"It is."

"Did you get it for this occasion?" Luke asks curiously.

"I did," I say, returning his smile. I figure the detail about my best friends buying it for me for precisely this occasion is probably more information than he needs.

He slips his arm around my back and into my sopping wet hair, turning my face toward his. I look at him, taking inventory of his brown eyes, his thick black eyelashes, and his honey-colored skin with a smattering of freckles on his nose. I memorize his pink lips, which turn up at the corners even when he isn't smiling. He lets me stare at him, waiting for me, as though I'm rereading the last chapter of my favorite book and he's allowing me to enjoy those final precious words.

When I've fully taken him in, I lean forward to kiss him. He kisses me back with several tiny kisses. I lie back on the blanket, pulling him on top of me, opening my mouth as though I'm inviting his tongue in to play. The kissing becomes deeper, more intense, hungrier. He reaches between us to remove the towel that is awkwardly tangled in our legs. Once the towel has been cast aside, we lie there, two warm clean bodies fused together, legs and tongues intertwined, skin welcoming as much contact as possible.

The only barrier between us is the thin lacy silk of my lingerie. Luke moves in a gentle rocking motion and my body responds like he's leading me in a simple, rhythmic dance. I feel him get harder and harder. He shifts himself so he's lying next to me, giving him room to explore my body. With one hand propping up his head, his other hand starts at my neck and works its way down.

He pulls my straps down over my shoulders so that the nightgown is now bunched around my waist. He spends sufficient time tickling and rubbing my boobs, moving his hand from one to the other, circling each nipple with care. As his hand moves down my torso, he lets his mouth take over where his hand left off, sucking on my breasts and flicking his tongue against my nipples. My nipples harden, my breathing quickens, and I feel moisture accumulating between my legs. The feelings are wildly intense. I am on fire, wanting him, craving him.

His hand now moves lower and his fingers gently touch me, making their way inside. Not too deep, just exploring the parts, feeling the wetness. My hips writhe in response, the tickling becoming almost unbearable. Now I have a deep need to have him inside me. I want him to fill me up and reach the depths of me.

"Does that feel good?" he whispers in my ear.

"Better than anything," I say through almost-gasps.

I suddenly become aware that he's doing all the work. I am lying on my back, one hand behind my head, the other in Luke's thick, soft hair. He is touching me, making me feel things I've never felt before, and I am not reciprocating at all. How is this supposed to work? Do we take turns or do it simultaneously?

I reach over and grab hold of him. He is hard and hot and poking straight up at me. My hands instinctively know what to do. I wrap one hand firmly around the base and use the other to tickle the rest. I keep both hands moving, working in a rhythm. He moans in my ear, which turns me on even more. He doesn't stop touching me while I work on him. Our lips and tongues are fully enmeshed as we touch each other all over.

"I think it's time," he says.

"Me too."

"Are you sure?"

"I've never been more sure about anything," I say.

"Are they in the pink bag?"

"Not anymore," I say. I stand up and the nightgown falls to the floor at my feet. I step over it and reach behind the sofa cushion for the condoms.

"Very sly," Luke says.

I bring both packages over to the blanket. "Do you have a preference?"

Luke grabs one without much scrutiny and tears the wrapper open.

"Wanna help?" he asks.

"I don't know how," I say.

"I'll show you," he says as he places the rubber disc at the top of his penis. "Now just unroll it."

I put my hands on the condom and stretch it down over him. Luke wraps his arms around me and eases me onto my back, his legs gently pushing mine apart. I feel the tip of him poking at me. I open my legs farther as Luke rocks slowly back and forth, reaching a little deeper with each gentle thrust. The moisture between my legs gets more obvious, allowing him to enter me push by push, millimeter by millimeter.

It does hurt, but at the same time, it's exhilarating. With each push, I feel increased pressure, but I don't want him to stop. As he gets deeper inside me, both the pleasure and the pain build. I am determined to focus on the pleasure.

He is rubbing me in all the right places. I know he's not all the way in yet. I can tell that he's being ever so careful to enter me incrementally. I open up for him, slowly allowing him to push right through me. I'm so turned on that the wetness allows him to glide in. Now we are pressed against each other, and our bodies fit together like the only pieces in a two-part puzzle.

He starts to thrust with more force, his hips moving back and forth as he props himself up on his elbows, his mouth never leaving mine. My hands explore his back and I can feel his muscles tensing as he pushes. He pulls his face an inch away from mine and opens his eyes to check on me.

"You okay?" he asks.

"Yeah," I whisper.

"Feel good?"

"Feels so good," I answer.

My hands find his ass and squeeze while he moves up and down, in and out.

"I love you," he says.

"I love you back," I say.

His hips start to move faster, his breath getting quicker.

"Oh god," he says. "Oh, Janey."

I watch his face.

"I'm getting close," he tells me.

"Okay," I say. "I want to watch you."

His eyes close and he seems to drift to a far-off place. His mouth opens wide and I feel him throb inside me. It takes him a moment or two to return to our present, and he fully grasps the fact that I have been watching him while he climaxed. It's the first time I've ever noticed a hint of self-consciousness in Luke Hallstrom. He kisses me quickly and rolls next to me.

"That was unbelievable."

"It was?" I ask.

Luke looks offended. "You don't think so?"

I laugh a little. "Of course I think so. It was amazing. But I have nothing to compare it to," I say.

"Trust me," he says. "It was phenomenal."

"I'm glad," I say.

"You're not done, are you?" he asks.

"What do you mean?"

"You didn't have an orgasm."

"I don't think so, but I'm not sure," I say.

"What do you mean you're not sure?" he asks.

"I don't think I've ever had an orgasm," I say.

"Haven't you ever given yourself one?"

"No," I say, embarrassed.

"You should."

"You're telling me to masturbate?" I ask, incredulous.

"Well, yeah," he says, smiling, but completely serious.

"Why do I need to masturbate if I have you?"

"Because if you know what you like, I can do it for you," he says, as though it's the most obvious explanation ever.

"Okay," I say without really meaning it.

"Here, I'll help." He reaches his hand down and starts touching me again. "Tell me when I get to a good spot." He rubs back and forth, covering the whole area with rapid movements.

"Is that good?"

"That's really good," I say, leaning my head back and closing my eyes.

He keeps at it, moving more quickly, applying more pressure. The feeling starts to build, radiating from between my legs to my entire torso, down my legs, up my back.

"Have I found the spot?"

"Yes," I eke out.

"Want me to stop?" he teases.

"No," I say in the faintest of whispers.

I arch my back. I feel my knees shake. The feeling

grows almost intolerable. I let out an audible gasp as the orgasm takes hold of my entire body. After a brief recovery, I open my eyes to find Luke looking down at me.

"I think I came," I say, smiling.

"Yeah, I think so too," he says.

CHAPTER THIRTY-ONE

I FEEL DIFFERENT. I feel like a full-fledged woman. I now know what all the fuss is about. I am in on the joke. In my dad's apartment building, I was in an elevator full of adults, and I realized that everyone in that elevator had probably had sex. Including me. Now when I hear a song like Walk the Moon's "Jenny" and Nicholas Petricca sings, *Jenny's got a body just like an hourglass. I want to be the sand inside that hourglass,* I know what he's talking about. I know!

The morning after my first time, I wake up in my old bed, in my old room, in my old sheets, in my old faded pajamas, but I feel like a new person. I could swear when I catch my reflection in the mirror that I look a little different. Like it is written all over my face. It's as though I've gained an awareness that exudes from my every pore. However, while I am certain my newfound status as a non-virgin is somewhat obvious, I do love walking around like I'm holding a secret. A wonderful, personal secret.

Of course I share the details of my so-called secret

with Danielle and Sloan. I tell them about the car ride to my dad's place, the shower, and the first orgasm of my life (hopefully the first of many). I also tell them that while I had thought I was in love with Luke before we did it, the feelings I have for him now have intensified exponentially.

As we sit on the floor of Danielle's bedroom and I wax philosophic about the gravity of the sexual experience, I look at Sloan and see that there are tears in her eyes.

"What's the matter?" I ask Sloan, worried that I've been somehow insensitive or selfish. "Did I say something wrong?"

"No," Sloan says, dabbing at her eyes with the cuff of her sweatshirt. "I'm so happy for you."

"Then why are you crying?" I ask.

"I'm not crying," she says, her voice cracking and her tears dripping down her face more rapidly. We all share a giggle, and Danielle rubs Sloan's back.

"What's going on?" Danielle asks soothingly.

"I want my first time to be perfect," Sloan says, grabbing a tissue from the bedside table.

"Then it will be," I say.

"But I'm worried that I've already done too much."

"That's crazy," Danielle says. "Lots of people have hookups that end up meaning nothing. Your first time is still your first time, and nothing else matters."

"Maybe it will matter to the guy I fall in love with," Sloan says. "Maybe he'll want someone more pure."

"Then he's a dumbass," Danielle says. "Everything

you've done makes you who you are. And you're amazing."

"The guy who gets to be your first is so lucky," I add.

"You think?" Sloan asks, unsure.

"One hundred percent," Danielle says. "Whoever he is will get the benefit of a girl with experience along with the privilege of being your first."

Sloan seems to be lost in thought for a moment. "I'm changing my motto from *everything but* to *nothing but,*" Sloan says.

Danielle and I are now thoroughly confused.

"What?" Danielle asks.

"You're going to do nothing but have sex?" I ask.

"I'm not going to do anything with any guy until I am with someone I really care about. Someone I think is going to be the one," Sloan says. "I'm going to wait for something that feels real and good."

"I love that plan," Danielle says.

"That way," Sloan says, "I won't just have sex, I'll . . . *make love.*" She says it with exaggerated sappiness, emphasizing exactly what we all hate about that expression. We laugh and I push Sloan so she falls back onto the carpet.

I spend a lot of time thinking about Sloan, her regrets, and her determination to wipe the slate clean. Sloan can be whatever she wants to be, and she doesn't owe anyone an explanation. Sex undoubtedly means different things to people at different points in their lives. Aren't we all still figuring out who we want to be? Just a few short months ago, I had never been kissed and had no plans for romance. I never could have predicted the turn my life has taken.

Luke changed my self-awareness and my feelings about my own sexuality. For me, sex not only feels really good on a primal level, but it also makes me feel so much closer to Luke emotionally. I feel like I've given Luke a piece of myself that no one else will ever know.

Finding places to have sex is not easy. We can't just do it whenever and wherever we want. I don't feel right about going into Luke's bedroom and closing the door when his parents are home, and his mom is usually home. My dad has not taken any overnight trips recently, and my mom's house is just not an option. Since we're in the middle of track season, practices last until almost six p.m., and my mom expects me to walk in the door shortly thereafter. In fact, since I've been dating Luke, my mom seems acutely aware of the exact number of minutes it takes me to get home from school. I wonder if she suspects that Luke and I are trying to sneak in a quickie. She's so aware of my every move at every moment. Maybe she's ultra-focused on me because she's not with anyone right now. I do wonder when she last had sex. Scratch that. I don't want to know.

I have not told my mom that Luke and I have done it, but I have not told her that we *haven't*. I'm fairly certain she assumes it's happening, but I don't really feel the need to confirm or deny. Do we even have to have that conversation? After all, she is aware that I have a boyfriend and have purchased condoms. One could make an educated guess.

Despite the lack of readily available locations, Luke and I have still found the occasional time and place to be together. There have been the random (and amazing) weekend afternoons when his parents were playing golf and we took a break from studying to climb under his goose-down comforter. Also, Zach had a party when his parents were out of town, and Luke and I spent most of the party in the guest bedroom, his phone playing Red Hot Chili Peppers loud enough to cover the sounds of the party emanating from the backyard. We tried to ignore that the sheets smelled strongly of Zach's grandparents' Bengay.

Where there's a will, there's a way is Luke's mantra, and I fully support it.

CHAPTER THIRTY-TWO

*L*IFE WITH LUKE has found a rhythm, no pun intended. Even though I no longer question what he's doing with me, it still takes me by surprise when he tells me all the things he loves about me. He's constantly reminding me that I'm different from other girls. Special.

I guess it will take a while to undo the years of my considering myself ordinary. When I catch his gaze in the school hallway, or on the track, or at the lunch tables, a bolt of electricity shoots through my veins, landing squarely between my legs. He turns me on from afar, with merely the glint in his eye.

One rainy day in March, as track season is nearing its end, we have a quick workout in the weight room. Chow goes easy on us and dismisses practice more than an hour earlier than usual. As much as I want to go somewhere cozy and be alone with Luke, I know I should take advantage of the free time to work on my SAT prep.

Luke gives me a ride home, and the whole way from

school to my driveway, his hand slowly works its way up my thigh. He moves so incrementally that I barely notice the progress, but by the time he shuts off the Jeep's engine, his hand is between my legs, over my sweats, turning me on big-time. I lean back in the seat, spread my knees, lift my hips, and let him slide his hand down my sweats, beneath my underwear. I'm already completely wet, and having his fingers down there makes me long to have him inside me for real. I know we can't take this into the house, because my mom's car is parked in the driveway, serving as a barrier to entry.

Luke presses the release buttons on both of our seat belts and leans over to kiss me. I open my mouth and twirl my tongue in his mouth while I reach down to touch him. His erection is trapped inside his compression shorts. I pull the waistband down to free him from the Spandex restraint. We work on each other simultaneously while our tongues twist and turn in each other's mouths. I feel my breathing quicken while the sensation inside me builds. He knows exactly where to touch me, how fast to move, and how firmly to press to make me absolutely crazy.

I keep stroking him while I feel myself get hotter and closer. I can feel him get harder while my hand moves up and down.

"Are you close?" he whispers in my ear.

"How can you tell?" I ask through labored breathing.

"Your knees are shaking. They always shake when you're close."

"I'm almost there," I say.

He takes that as a cue to kick it up a notch, working a little faster and harder. Within seconds, the feelings overtake me and my moans drown out the sound of the raindrops beating on the Jeep's roof. After I recuperate, I can focus solely on him. I use both hands to cover every inch of him. We shift so that he sits back in his seat and I lean over him, kissing him while I tickle and stroke. Just as he knows how to make me burst, I know what he likes. I know where he likes me to be gentle and where he wants more pressure.

"Oh god," he mutters. His utterance of *Oh god* is the equivalent of my shaking knees. It's the signal to me that he is closing in. I pull my face away from his to watch his expression. I love to watch the ecstasy take over—his eyes squeeze shut and his mouth opens wide and he stays like that for a beat while he throbs in my hand.

He opens his eyes and sees that I was watching him progress through the stages of his orgasm. It's really the only time the formidable Luke Hallstrom is vulnerable. I like that he's surprisingly unaware of himself in that moment. I know that when he clears a high jump or executes a long jump, he is wholly in control of his body. He has been videoed by coaches and trainers, and photographed for yearbooks and school newspapers, so he has been able to examine and memorize how he appears in almost every scenario of his life. But he does not know what he looks like when he climaxes. I do.

"Why do you watch me?" he asks curiously.

"It makes me happy to see you experience pleasure," I say. "What's wrong with that?"

"I don't know. Nothing, I guess," he says. I sense his slight embarrassment.

"In case you forgot, I'm still kinda new at this," I say teasingly. "It's fascinating."

"Well, being with someone comfortable enough to watch me closely while I have an orgasm is new for me," he says.

"If it helps," I say playfully, "when you're in ecstasy, you're more handsome than ever."

Luke laughs. "Oh, thank god. I was so worried."

After straightening myself up and kissing Luke goodbye, I walk into the house, still much earlier than I would have if we had had a regular track workout. I plan to give my mom a quick kiss, answer her usual *How was school today?* questions, and move on to an SAT practice test.

My mom is not in the kitchen or the den, so I plop my backpack on my bedroom floor and walk the five steps down the hall to what used to be my parents' room. Her door is partially closed, so I give it a push and am confused and mystified by the sight before me. Clothes, including a dorky pair of Reebok sneakers, have been discarded haphazardly. Two naked bodies are moving feverishly atop the champagne-colored duvet. My mother is on her back amid her throw pillows, her legs splayed. An unknown man is on top of her, his back slightly hairy and his bald spot evident, even in the dim light of the rainy afternoon. His ass, also slightly hairy, knocks repeatedly against my mother, and with each knock, she lets out a little grunt. It takes me a second or two to make sense of what I'm seeing. My mom is having sex. My mother is having raucous, furious, daytime sex in my parents' bed with a man who most definitely is not my father.

What the hell do I do now? I would like to vomit and run away. In that order. But instead I just stand here, unable to move. I have never seen two other people entwined in sexual intercourse. Either my parents really didn't do it with any frequency, or they were very careful about protecting me from these horrific images. It is, without question, the grossest thing I have ever witnessed. Perhaps the tableau before me is particularly revolting because it's my mother. Or because it's my mother and hairy-ass Reebok man. Or simply because heated, energetic, matinee sex is really not meant to be viewed by a third party. I have to get out of here, so I take one backward step—and bump into the half-open door.

The two of them jump apart so quickly that I think my naked mother is going to hit the ceiling. Hairy-ass

Reebok man grabs a pillow and covers his crotch. I run. I hear my mom calling my name, but I can't stick around to listen to whatever else she has to say. I grab my purse and the car key from the hook by the front door and leave the house as fast as I possibly can.

CHAPTER THIRTY-THREE

I TEXT LUKE as I race out the door to the car: *Can I come over?* I start the engine, put on my seat belt, and see his response: *Sure. Everything ok?* I don't take the time to text back. I just hightail it over to his house as fast as I can, trying like mad to scrub the gruesome pictures from my brain.

Luke lets me into his kitchen, where he is feasting on a snack of leftover fried chicken, half a cantaloupe, and a carton of yogurt. This is merely his afternoon snack. In a couple of hours, he will be hungry enough to inhale a three-course meal lovingly made by his mother or the housekeeper, whatever we choose to believe.

"What's wrong?" he asks.

"I walked in on my mother having sex," I pant.

He lets out a burst of laughter. "You can't unsee that!"

"Tell me about it," I say.

"Who was she having sex with?"

"I don't know. He has a bald spot and a hairy ass."

"He should take some of the hair off his ass and put it on his head." Luke keeps laughing.

"Be serious," I beg. "I'm in full crisis mode."

"Why?" he asks, scooping out a big piece of orange flesh from the cantaloupe.

"*Why?*" I mimic incredulously. "*Why? Are you hear-ing me? My mother was screwing some random guy. In the middle of the afternoon. In my parents' bedroom. I am freaking out."

"Okay," he says, trying to be serious, but unable to wipe the grin from his face, "I get that it's not something anyone should ever see. And it must be really weird for you, but . . ." he trails off.

"But what?" I demand.

"Good for her," he says.

"Are you kidding?" I ask in sheer disbelief.

"No," he says. "Want some chicken?" he asks, holding up a drumstick.

I shake my head. He takes a bite and wipes his face with a napkin. "Look, I get it. It's traumatic to see your mom doing it. I walked in on my parents once. I was eleven years old, and I still remember every detail. Not pretty."

"And this wasn't even my dad," I add.

"Yeah, I get that, too. It's really disturbing. But putting that aside, aren't you a little happy for your mom?"

"Not even a little bit," I say, surprised that we're on such vastly different planes here.

"So you can and she can't?" he asks.

"What do you mean?" I press.

"You're having sex. It's great, right? Don't you think she should be able to have a little fun, too?"

I sit down next to him at the kitchen table and try to speak as calmly as possible.

"She's supposed to be the parent, the sensible one. She was having sex in broad daylight, and her bedroom door wasn't even closed, let alone locked. That's not acting like the responsible parent."

"I guess she didn't think you were coming home," he rationalizes.

I get more and more aggravated that he seems only to be looking at things from my mom's perspective. He has yet to express any empathy for me. "Even so," I say. "She was careless and selfish."

"Okay. What else?" he asks.

"What do you mean, *what else?*" I ask, not making any effort to mask how annoyed I am.

"What exactly are you freaking out about?" he asks.

"Well, who is this guy? She hasn't told me that she's seeing anyone or is interested in anyone or has gone on a single date."

"Have you told her?" he asks.

"Have I told her what?" I ask him.

"That you've had sex," he says.

"No," I say.

He gives me a look that says *See, two can play at that game.*

"You're taking her side," I say. I realize how immature I sound. But I can't help myself.

"I'm only pointing out that you're not talking to her about stuff, but you expect her to come clean to you," he says.

I am the one on the debate team, but Luke seems to be winning this argument, and it's making me insane. He's calm and direct and thoughtful, just as I try to be when I am debating. I, on the other hand, am passionate and upset and thoroughly frazzled. Not effective in persuasive speaking. I try a new approach.

"Here's the difference. I am in a committed relationship. Whereas this guy with bad shoes and a hairy ass could mean absolutely nothing to her."

"Big deal," he says.

"It is a big deal!" I practically shout.

Luke gets up and puts the food away. He rinses his dish in the sink and places it in the dishwasher. He takes his empty glass, fills it with water, comes back to the table, and puts the glass of water in front of me. "Here," he says. "Drink some water and calm down."

Being told to calm down has never actually compelled anyone to calm down. It tends to have the opposite effect.

"Why is it so bad?" he wants to know.

"You want to know why it's so bad that my mother is having meaningless sex?" I ask him.

"I do," he says matter-of-factly. "She's a big girl. She

should be able to do what she wants. I would think that now that you know how good sex is, you would be less uptight about it."

Oh snap! Did he just call me uptight? I take a deep breath and gather my thoughts. I try to put him on the defensive.

"I guess I just think that sex should mean something. I thought you felt the same way. Guess I was wrong."

He is remarkably unruffled. "I think sometimes casual sex is okay."

I worry that our conversation has taken a turn and we are no longer talking about my mom. Maybe now we're talking about us. "When would be one of those times where you are a big fan of casual sex?" I ask, my emotions taking hold of me.

"It depends," he says, cleverly staying as vague as possible. My mind starts to race to next September. Luke will be three thousand miles away, going to parties and making the most of his newfound freedom. That will probably be one of the times when casual sex makes sense to him. I beg myself not to say something I'm going to regret. I do not want to sound whiny and jealous and needy and possessive. *Don't say it, Janey, don't say it . . .*

"Freshman year of college, perhaps?" Damn! I have no self-control.

"What about it?" he asks, but I think he knows exactly what I'm talking about.

"Would freshman year of college be the right occasion for hookups?" I ask, fully committed to the dangerous destination to which I've taken our disagreement.

"Again," he says, "it depends." His words and demeanor do not convey any emotion. He's remaining very lighthearted and refusing to take the bait and make this personal. It's driving me a little nuts.

"Right," I say, gaining strength to press him for an answer that is only going to rip my heart open. "But, generally speaking, would you agree with that statement?"

Luke takes a deep breath. Grabs my water and drinks it down.

"Hey, what we have is great. It's the best thing ever, but we have to admit that things change. We'd be crazy to try to keep this up next year. Long-distance relationships never work, and you should have a blast your senior year."

He said it. It's out there. We are going to break up when he leaves. I guess I always knew it, but hearing him say it out loud cuts through to my soul. And yet he tries to spin the bad news as though it's going to be really great for me.

"Don't put this on me. I'm not looking to have a blast. I'm not the one who is a big proponent of the empty hookup. That seems to be your department."

"Janey, you're getting really emotional."

"No shit," I say. Now I'm pissed and I am not trying to hide it. "Sorry if this is an emotional subject for me. I happen to think sex requires emotion. Guess you don't."

"You sound really judgy," he says. He has run out of patience. His tone is turning cold.

"Oh, I'd hate to *judge* you for all the nameless, faceless sex you're planning," I say with all the sarcasm I can muster. "You know what? Why wait? Feel free to start now." I grab my keys and walk out his front door, trying not to cry.

CHAPTER THIRTY-FOUR

OW IS THIS HAPPENING? How are the people I thought I knew transforming before my very eyes? Is Mercury in retrograde (whatever that means)? I ran to Luke to ease the shock and horror of witnessing my presumed-to-be-celibate mom in the throes of appalling passion, only to be made aware that he's not so committed to this commitment thing. Here I am, annoyingly confident that sex in a real relationship is the only way to go, that I've given Luke a piece of myself and that I'm so fortunate that my first experience is something real. And the truth is that my boyfriend (is he even my boyfriend anymore?) has much different views about sex than I do. And much different views than I thought he did.

Less than an hour ago, we were zealously bringing each other to orgasm in his Jeep, and now our relationship status is questionable and our future seemingly nonexistent. Would it have been so hard for him to be sympathetic? Couldn't he have just said, *Aw, man, Janey, that sucks.*

I can't believe your mom would do it with a random stranger. I would never do it with a random stranger. Well, maybe not exactly like that, but something along those lines. I mean, sometimes it's okay just to tell someone what she needs to hear, isn't it?

I can't go home quite yet. The idea of facing my mother is just too excruciating to consider. If I thought the *How was your day, sweetie?* questions were grating, I can only imagine what she has in store for me now. Perhaps if I stay out late enough, she'll be asleep when I get home. If I'm lucky, she'll be exhausted from all the high-octane afternoon activity.

Sloan. Sloan is the answer here. Sloan has a new job at a pizza place in La Jolla Village Square. She is planning to go on a student tour of London and Paris this summer, and her parents are asking her to pay for half of the trip. This is her first week on the job and she's been working really hard. I walk in, grab a table, and wait for her to notice I'm there. She catches sight of me from behind the counter, where she's working the cash register. I don't want to interrupt her or get her in trouble, so I wait. When she gets her break, we take a walk around the mall. I fill her in on the unfortunate, and unsightly, recent events. Sloan, my port in the storm, has all the right answers.

"What is your mother thinking?" she asks, incensed. "She went all holy and pure when she found your condoms, and meanwhile she's got a little something going on? Who is she to tell you that you don't know Luke well enough to do it? Does she even know this guy? I mean, who is he?"

"Exactly!" I concur, thankful to finally be in the presence of sanity. What a relief it is to speak to someone who validates my feelings. "And Sloan, it was so unbelievably gross. I mean, the sights, the sounds, the whole thing. I can't shake the image."

"Ugh! I can only imagine. It's making me sick, and I didn't even see it."

"Seriously," I say as we sit on a bench outside the movie theater. "But the worst part is Luke. It's almost like he took the opportunity to say, 'By the way, your mom's not the only one who's going to be surprising you with terrible news today. I, too, plan to sleep with people who mean nothing to me.'"

"I'm shocked. I thought he was so into the committed-relationship thing," she says.

"I thought so too," I say. "But he seems to think there are plenty of wonderful opportunities to have sex with perfect strangers. He definitely does not see this lasting after he's gone."

"Very disappointing," Sloan says, checking the time on her phone. "I gotta get back."

"Don't make me go home," I whine teasingly. "I can't face my horny mommy."

I walk Sloan back to work. She gives me a big hug. "Just tell her she's your role model and you want to be just like her, so you're going to take a page out of her playbook, and she might want to knock on your bedroom door from here on out." We share a laugh.

"Excellent idea," I say. "What would I do without you?"

I walk into the house as quietly as is humanly possible, hoping and praying that I can somehow avoid a confrontation. I have barely placed a foot inside when I hear her.

"Hi, honey," she says. Her voice is lacking that chipper tone she usually uses when she's greeting me at the end of the day. She's taking a more careful, almost apologetic approach. "I'm in the kitchen. Come on in."

Is *No thanks, I'm good* an option? Probably not. I enter cautiously. I half expect my mom to look different somehow. My impression of her has changed so dramatically since I saw her this afternoon, legs spread and bouncing furiously, that I am pleasantly surprised to find my unchanged mother at the stove.

Mom is stirring a big pot of minestrone soup. Warm crusty bread and a chopped salad are already on the table. She's prepared one of my favorite meals—her shameless attempt to win me back, no doubt. The table is set for two. Trapped!

"I'm not really hungry," I say, hoping she'll let me retreat into the safety of my room.

"Sit down, Janey," she says, sweetly but firmly.

"Is there any chance we can get away with not discussing this?" I ask, almost begging.

"No chance," my mom says. She gives me a remorseful smile. "Sit down."

I do as I'm told and sit at the table while my mom doles out bowls of soup. I toss the salad and load generous heaps onto our plates even though I feel far too nauseated to digest chopped turkey, salami, and cheese. However, assuming the duty of salad server does afford me the opportunity to look at something other than my mother's *We're about to have a very important conversation* expression.

She sits down and wastes no time. "I'm very sorry about this afternoon."

"Not half as sorry as I am," I say.

"I can only imagine how surprising that was for you," she adds, trying to be sympathetic.

"Can you, Mom? Can you, really?" I don't know if she really grasps how utterly horrific it was for me.

"Yes, I can," she tries to assure me.

"Who even was that?" I ask.

"Jason Maiser," she explains. "He's a fifth-grade teacher. He's new this year. He's been divorced about a year, has two kids in college—"

"I don't need his résumé," I interrupt. "How long have you been seeing him?"

"We've gone out a couple of times," she says, breaking off a piece of bread and putting it on her plate.

"A couple of times? Do you know him well enough to have sex?" I ask pointedly.

"I don't think that's really your business," she says,

clearly trying not to sound punishing, but it stings none-theless.

I take a big swallow of soup. "That's essentially what you said to me when you were worried I was rushing into sex with Luke," I say.

"It's different," she says.

"How is it different?" I want to know.

Mom puts down her spoon and leans back in her chair. "I'm a grown woman. A woman going through a divorce. You're still technically a kid. And you're *my* kid, so it's my job to try to guide you in the right direction. I want you to make good choices that you won't regret."

"But you should be taking your own advice," I say. "You should be making good choices. After all, as you say, you're a grownup, so you should behave like one."

"Are you saying that grownups shouldn't have sex?" she asks.

"No. Of course not. I know grownups have sex. But I don't think you should be having sex with some dude from work you barely know. And in the afternoon with your door open? Seriously, Mom, not so *grown-up* of you," I say.

"Okay, I'll give you that. Yes, it was stupid to assume you weren't coming home and to be careless about the time and place. However, I want to remind you that long-ing and desire and need do not go away when you hit thirty or forty, or probably fifty," she says, looking closely at me.

"This may be falling into the category of too much information," I caution, getting up from the table to refill my soup bowl.

"I don't think so," she says. "Teenagers tend to assume that the world, and all the good stuff in it, is reserved for them. But Janey, when you're thirty-five and forty, you're going to feel like the same person you feel like today. And you're still going to want to feel wanted. That doesn't go away."

"I'm not saying it goes away, but I would think that your priorities would change. I mean, isn't being a mom, *being my mom,* more important than getting some?"

Now she looks confused. "Well, first, don't be gross. And second, of course it is. Nothing is more important to me than being your mom. But I'm not *just* your mom. I'm also a woman. A woman who is single for the first time in almost twenty years." She puts down her fork and shifts her body so she's leaning on the table, her face getting close to mine. "Let me ask you this," she says. "How do you feel when you're with Luke?"

"I'm not sure what you're asking me," I say. I'm afraid she wants me to talk about how he makes me feel sexually, and there's no way in hell I'm going there.

"When you're walking down the street and his arm is around you. Or when he sends you a text and tells you he loves you. How does that make you feel?"

"Um, good?" I answer weakly.

"Come on, Janey, you've mastered the English language, for god's sake. I would think you'd be able to come up with something a little more descriptive than just one syllable. Tell me how it makes you feel to know that this guy who is smart and athletic and handsome adores you. Think about it."

I think about Luke. I think about the first time he held my hand in the school hallway. I think about our first kiss in his Jeep after we had smoothies. I think about the time he stood me in front of my mirror and told me I was perfect.

"I feel lucky and beautiful," I admit.

"Do you think you're ever going to stop wanting to feel that?" she asks.

I think for an extended moment. This time not about Luke, but about myself. The way I feel about myself has changed considerably since that fateful plane ride from Mexico to San Diego. I am aware of myself as a sexual person who is desired. I am confident about the woman I am becoming. I love how I feel.

"No." I sigh.

The past few months have brought more changes and surprises and challenges than the several years prior. My parents' separation has made me redefine our family. As a kid, I thought of my parents as merely a mom and a dad, like they had no other identities. Sure, I was aware of their jobs, but their roles of teacher and pilot were secondary to their jobs of meeting my needs. My needs to be fed, driven, tickled, tucked in, read to, hugged, kissed, cheered up, and advised. My mom and dad met all of my needs—physical, material, emotional—readily and appropriately. I didn't ever stop to think that those needs are not unique to me. They are basic human needs, and my parents, as hard as it is to admit, are human.

I can now fully understand that part of growing up is accepting that my parents are grownups, and grownups are complex human beings who have not only needs, but also shortcomings and flaws. They mess up, just like I do. I'm not going to stop messing up just because I get married and have kids. Even though my mom and dad look and act, in my eyes, like old people, I guess they don't feel much different than they did when they were seventeen. They're working hard to meet my needs as well as their own.

I have fallen in love and become aware of an array of new and pressing needs. I now feel the need to be touched and pleased. Knowing what it feels like to be truly wanted has made me realize that I need that, too. It's scary to need something that I cannot provide for myself. It makes me feel vulnerable to know that these emotions that are making me feel whole could go away.

Luke makes me feel sexy and strong and desired. And he's going away. Does that mean those feelings are going to go away? I don't want to feel complete only when there's a boy around who loves me. I won't always have a boyfriend. I don't *want* to always have a boyfriend. I want to be single and independent at various times throughout my life, and I need to be okay with that. I need to figure out how to keep feeling confident even when no one is holding me close and whispering *I love you* into my ear.

It makes my head spin to imagine the future, how I'm going to feel, what I'm going to want. I'm not ready to think like a grownup, even though I'm well aware that what I'm doing with Luke is supposedly a pretty grown-up thing. Right this very second I feel like a little kid— lost and untethered. The afternoon was confusing and up-setting. I hate that I saw my mother having sex. I hate that I fought with Luke. I hate that I'm going to lose him. I have so many feelings inside me, feelings that are new and complicated. I'm scared.

What I think I really need right now is my mom. Or, more accurately, my mommy. I want the mommy who makes me feel safe and snug, not the person I saw doing the horizontal bop this afternoon. I want to crawl next to her in her big comfy bed and watch reruns of *Friends* like we used to do when I was in middle school and my dad was away. Back then, I didn't think about sex, my mother's or mine. Ross and Rachel's romance was the only sex that mattered at the time.

From my bedroom, I hear my mom's shower turn off. I know she's probably wrapping her hair in a towel and put-ting on her thick white terry-cloth robe. I cast my home-work aside and pad down the hallway to my mom's room. "I'll Be There for You" is already playing in my head.

CHAPTER THIRTY-FIVE

SPRING BREAK. Danielle's parents and brothers will be at a lacrosse tournament in Orange County, and Danielle invited me to spend a few days with her at her grandparents' house in Palm Springs. The opportunity to get out of town was too good to pass up. Sadly, Sloan has to stay home and work at the pizza place. Brett wanted to come with us, but Danielle's grandmother said no boys allowed. Too bad; I would have loved some chill time with Brett.

Luke flew to Boston by himself to visit his brother and sister. Things have been strained and awkward between us since our fight in his kitchen. We haven't spent any real time together, and we haven't addressed the issue of our looming expiration date. I'm honestly not sure where we stand.

The night before we left for the desert, Danielle was at Charlie's house. He was in the shower and she was playing Candy Crush in his room. Charlie's phone, which was near Danielle on Charlie's bed, was lighting up with text messages. Out of curiosity, she picked up his phone, only to see a text from some girl he met in summer camp four years ago. The girl's name is Eve, she lives in San Francisco, and she sent very graphic messages about all the things she wanted to do to Charlie in bed. Danielle scrolled through the history and found that this pornographic conversation had been going on for weeks. Charlie reciprocated the sexting, offering up his fantasies and desires as well.

"He told her he wanted to squirt whipped cream all over her and lick it off," Danielle told me. "Charlie and I did that on Valentine's Day. It was my idea."

Charlie came out of the shower, wearing a towel. He approached Danielle and dropped the towel, revealing a boner and an urgent need for sex. Danielle looked at his penis, then up at Charlie, and said, "Maybe Eve would like to take care of that for you." Charlie quickly lost his erection, his mojo, and his girlfriend.

In Palm Springs, Danielle and I do some much-needed relaxing. For four days, we sleep late, then get iced coffees and bring them to the pool in her grandparents' backyard. We swim and tan all day long, only going inside to eat the tuna sandwiches and cookies her grandmother makes us for lunch.

Every afternoon, we FaceTime with Sloan, who seems to be gunning for Employee of the Month. She's taken on extra hours and swears she hasn't been to a single party since we've been gone.

"No boy action?" Danielle asks her.

"Nope," Sloan answers swiftly.

"So what have you been doing after work?" I ask.

"Not much," she says. "Just chilling."

Later, Danielle and I discuss how impressed we are that Sloan has been so committed to putting in the hours at work. She also seems to be avoiding parties and doing stuff with boys she would probably end up regretting. I guess she meant it when she promised herself she'd wait for a guy who means something.

"Not that there's anything wrong with hooking up," I say, smiling, trying to shed the *uptight* moniker Luke attached to me.

"Honestly, I think I could go for a meaningless hookup right about now," Danielle admits.

I'm surprised that Danielle seems so strangely unaffected by her breakup with Charlie. She doesn't appear to be unhappy or wounded at all.

"Maybe I was ready," Danielle admits. "Things were getting kind of boring."

"Still," I say, "it had to piss you off when you found those texts."

"Oh my god, yes," she admits. "I wanted to kill him. But mostly because it was a blow to my ego, not because I was heartbroken. We were bickering a lot, and he just isn't as funny as he thinks he is." It's true. Charlie does try to entertain everyone with his often nonexistent wit. It can get tiresome.

"So you can just move on? It's that easy?" I ask.

"No, of course not. I'm thinking about him a lot. But I don't really miss him, and that's how I know it was time to break up. Whatever he was doing with this Eve person was probably for the same reasons. It was time to end it, but neither of us knew how."

"Wow," I say. "You're so well-adjusted."

"I think I want a little taste of the single life," Danielle says. I can see that Danielle is ready for a change. Ready to experience something new and different.

Everything Danielle says about Charlie is the opposite of how I feel about Luke. I miss him terribly, and I don't think it's time for us to end things. And, probably most important of all, Luke was absolutely right. He was right that sometimes people need sex with no strings attached. As hard as it is to admit, my mom is a woman who is coming out of a marriage that lacked a spark. She deserves to have some crazy, grownup fun, even if it throws my worldview into a tailspin. Danielle, too, is ready for a fling without a commitment. People need different kinds of sex and affection at different times of their lives.

Right now, I need Luke. He and I will be going our separate ways, but for now, the spark still sparkles, so why extinguish it before we have to? Why push something away that makes me so happy? I grab my phone and send him a text: *I miss you.*

A few minutes go by, during which I agonize about

the fact that he hasn't replied. What does it mean? He doesn't miss me? He's already moving on? Then I realize that it's eleven P.M. in Palm Springs, which means it's two a.m. in Boston. Maybe he's asleep. I must convince myself that he's asleep in order not to obsess about him and why he's not responding to my text.

Luke is going to leave right after he graduates, in just two short months. He will be three thousand miles away, meeting new people who are definitely going to find him as irresistible and captivating as I do, as everyone does. And Luke will win their hearts. I can see him now, everyone's best friend and the object of many girls' fantasies. I don't think I can stand it. It would make me insane to be in San Diego, knowing that Luke's charm is working its way around the greater Boston area. I can't try to hold on to him. It wouldn't work for either of us.

I will do my best to enjoy every morsel of Luke for the next two months, and then I'll let him go free. It'll be better that way. Better for my sanity.

Danielle and I watch *Pitch Perfect* for about the millionth time and then go to sleep.

In the morning, I wake before Danielle and I reach over to turn on my phone. The time it takes to power up is sheer agony. I make sure the phone is on silent and hold it under the blanket so that the light doesn't disturb Danielle.

Two texts. Both from Luke. The first one: *I miss you too.*

I miss you like crazy. I think about you all the time. I love you more than anything. I have one very important question. The second one: *Will you go to the prom with me?*

I let out a squeal that wakes Danielle out of her comatose slumber. Whoops.

CHAPTER THIRTY-SIX

I GET BACK FROM PALM SPRINGS a few days before Luke is due home from Boston. My time away has served to dissipate the awkwardness between my mother and me. I don't ask my mom what she was up to in the four days I was gone. I figure our new system for maintaining a happy house is *don't ask, don't tell*. The truth is, I really don't want to know.

Mom takes me shopping for a dress to wear to Luke's prom. I can't remember the last time my mom and I spent the day together. I am reminded that she's pretty fun to be with, and find that we desperately needed a little bonding time. We keep the conversation away from sex, unpleasant run-ins, prophylactics, Reeboks, and romance. We concentrate on the task at hand—the need to find the perfect dress. I have been informed that the general prom rule is that senior girls wear long gowns while younger girls, if they're lucky enough to be invited, wear shorter dresses.

At the department store, we take nearly twenty-five dresses into the fitting room. My mom serves as my dutiful attendant; she can get pieces on and off hangers in a flash. She immediately knows if a dress will or won't work, and she can tell when a stitch here or a hem there is the answer to a perfect fit. We laugh pretty hard when the saleswoman brings us dresses with bows, sequins, or ruffles. We both know that's never going to fly.

I fall in love with a shell-pink dream of a dress. It's delicate and beautiful—the ideal combination of adorable and sexy. The dress has spaghetti straps, a snug bodice, and a flouncy short skirt. Mom brilliantly pairs the dress with high-heeled, strappy silver sandals.

"Mom, it's all so expensive," I say. "I don't want you to spend too much."

"It's the prom." She says it as though it's my wedding. "And you're going to look so beautiful." She may be single and horny, but she hasn't lost the ability to be a doting, generous, sentimental mother who only wants the best for me.

I am picking Luke up at the airport on Saturday evening and I am strangely nervous, which I suppose is because we haven't seen each other in more than a week, and the last time we were together, things were tense to say the least. However, given our recent conversations, I'm confident that we're back on track. We haven't discussed the unresolved issues, but he told me he missed me and loved me and, at this point, that's good enough for me.

I get to the airport way too early and wait by my car at

the curb outside baggage claim. At long last, Luke emerges from the terminal, and the sight of him takes my breath away. Whenever I get off a plane, I feel slimy and disgusting, but Luke somehow looks like he's walking out of a catalog. His jeans, shirt, and hair are just the right amount of rumpled. I run up to him and throw my arms around him. He lifts me up and I bury my face in his neck. He also smells delicious despite spending the last six hours in a cylinder of germ-ridden, recirculated air. I can't keep my hands off him.

In the car on the way home from the airport, I tell Luke about my lazy days by the pool in Palm Springs. He tells me about his visit to Boston College and the dorm he hopes to get. I hear about the night Luke, his brother Jackson, and Jackson's boyfriend, Brady, went out and did karaoke. They drank beer and sang eighties pop songs all night.

We go back to my house, where I finally feel comfortable enough to be with Luke. I mean really *be* with Luke. Mom is out with Reebok hairy-ass man and she said, in no uncertain terms, that she wouldn't be home before eleven. I think she's allowing me a little freedom in order to enjoy some herself. Luke and I get back to my house and go directly to my room. Even though I know we'll be here alone for the next two hours, I still close my door.

"I missed you so much," Luke says, grabbing me around the waist and pulling me to him.

"I missed you too," I say. "So much." I reach up and

comb my fingers through his thick hair, which has gotten longer since we started dating, the waves a little messier.

He pushes me up against my bedroom door. His chest meets my chest, his hips meet my hips. Our lips find each other. The kisses start out soft, then turn hungry and urgent. He kisses my ear and down my neck to my collarbone.

"God, you smell good. I could eat you." He sighs.

I pull my shirt over my head, revealing a new purple bra I bought with this reunion in mind.

"Wow," he says. "Recent purchase?"

"Yep," I say. "It's for you." I then step out of my shorts to reveal a matching purple thong.

"You're killing me," Luke says, breathing heavily. "Turn around, let me see the full picture."

I give Luke a little twirl, showing him my new ensemble.

"Nice tan," he says.

"Come here," I say, pulling him to my bed. I push the stuffed animals onto my floor, not so much because I need to make room, but because I don't need reminders that I'm about to have sex in the same bed I once referred to as my "big-girl bed."

I lie down, still in my matching bra and thong. Luke whips off his shirt and then takes off his jeans and underwear in one fell swoop. He stands there wearing nothing but his leather braided bracelet, and I take in his body, dripping in flawlessness. I am aware how things have changed. I can now take the time to stare at him, every inch of him, for as long as I want. With the lights on, I lie on my bed, practically naked, and I'm happy to know he's looking at me as well.

He lies on top of me, his body covering mine. He wraps his arms around me, puts his hands under my butt, and presses me up to him. We kiss and kiss and kiss, our bodies moving in a syncopated rhythm. He moves his hands from my butt up my back and starts to take off my bra.

"I'll be right back," I say. I walk out of my room and close the door behind me.

In anticipation of seeing Luke, I bought something other than the new underwear. My time with Danielle inspired me. I walk into the dark kitchen and open the refrigerator. I reach up to the top shelf, behind the milk and orange juice, grab the red and white metal can, and hurry back to my room.

Luke is lying on the bed, his erection waiting eagerly for my return.

"Whatcha got there?" he asks, referring to the hand I hold behind my back.

"Ta-da!" I say, revealing the brand-new can of Reddi-wip.

Luke's eyes open wide. "What do you plan to do with that?" he asks, his eyes twinkling knowingly.

I sit on top of Luke, straddling him at his waist. I remove the red cap, point the plastic tip at his torso, and spray the white creamy sugar in a small mound on his chest.

"Ah! That's cold," he says with a laugh, and when the tip of his tongue peeks out, as it always does when he laughs, I spray a dab of whipped cream on it and then suck it off his tongue.

"What's gotten into you?" he wants to know. "The sexy purple stuff, the whipped cream. You've been planning."

"I've been thinking about you a lot," I say, and I spray the whipped cream in a straight line from his chest down to where his body hits mine. I lean down and lick him, using my tongue to cover his chest and stomach in the sugary goodness and then lick him clean. After I've worked over Luke's entire body, he takes the can from me and returns the favor.

He removes my bra and thong and instructs me to lie down. Luke is very strategic about his placement and has impressive control over the spray can. He puts a tiny dab behind my ear and licks my neck. He then squirts a little pile on each of my boobs and takes his sweet time making sure he gets all the whipped cream off my skin. It is nearly impossible to stay still when he draws a thin line down my side from my ribs to my hipbone. Instead of licking it clean, he delicately uses his tongue to make little waves in the white stream. I can barely stand it. I practically beg him to have sex with me.

"What's your hurry?" he asks teasingly.

"I can't take it anymore," I admit.

He puts the can down, swiftly puts on one of the condoms I placed on my nightstand, and lowers himself onto me. While he kisses me tenderly, he enters me. Our bodies are sticky from the whipped cream and every time he moves up and down, our skin clings together as if trying not to let go.

"Can we take a shower?" Luke asks when we're finished, indicating the mess of leftover whipped cream and sweat that is caked between us. I check the time and see that we still have plenty of time to ourselves.

I take him into my bathroom and hang two towels over the shower door. We step in and allow the hot water to wash away the remnants of the evening.

"That was incredible," he says. "I didn't know food and sex could be such a good combo."

"You've never experimented like that before?" I ask.

"Nope," he says. "Can't say that I have."

"Well, aren't you lucky to have me around to show you a thing or two?" I say with more than a hint of irony.

"I'm very lucky." He says it so sincerely that it seems he's no longer talking about whipped cream.

"Glad you enjoyed it," I say.

"You're full of surprises," he says, picking up the shampoo and squeezing some into his hand.

"I have another surprise," I say. He looks at me as if to ask, *What else can you possibly have up your sleeve?* Here goes. "You were right." I soap up my body and reach out to him to spread soap on his shoulders and arms.

"I was? About what?" he wants to know.

"That sometimes sex is just sex, and that's okay," I say.

"Where is this coming from?" I am aware of the oddity of the serious conversation we're having while standing in my shower.

"I've given it a lot of thought," I say. "The thing with my mom. She does deserve to live life fully and freely. And you're leaving for college soon. You should be free to make the most of that time as well."

"We don't have to think about that now," he says, rinsing the shampoo from his hair.

"I know, but I want you to know that I understand."

"Well, there's something else you should understand." He pulls me close so we stand under the hot stream together.

"Sex when you really care is better. Sex with you is the best I've ever had."

"It is?" I ask, overcome with relief.

"It is," he says.

CHAPTER THIRTY-SEVEN

THE LAST NIGHT of spring break, Danielle and Sloan and I have a plan to go bowling. We know the workload is about to get intense, and we figure this is our last chance to have some fun without tests and papers and projects hanging over our heads.

About an hour before we're set to meet at the bowling alley, I get a text from Brett:

What r u doing tonite?

Bowling with the girls, I respond.

Can I come? That's odd. Brett never wants to come out with Danielle, Sloan, and me. He complains that we have too many inside jokes, and he doesn't like all the yammering on about boys.

Really? U want to? I text back.

Nothing else to do, he types. I wonder what this is about. I really hope he's not going to spend the evening criticizing Luke and reminding me that he thinks I rushed into having sex with him. I have been entirely candid with Brett lately; there's no sense in keeping secrets, so I told him that Luke and I did it. The conversation went better than I thought it would. Brett was the good, supportive friend I had hoped he would be, and he kept the disapproval and criticism to a minimum. Or maybe he just kept it to himself.

I also told Brett that Luke and I hit a rough patch before break. I shared with him that it's clear my romance with Luke is not on the path to happily ever after. Maybe he wants to come tonight because he thinks there's a window of opportunity to finally convince me that guys like Luke are a waste of time and space. God, I hope not. Brett and I have just gotten back to the place where we're comfortable enough around each other to speak freely and openly again.

I fire off a text to Sloan and Danielle to ask if they're okay with Brett crashing. Within seconds, Sloan responds *Sure*. Danielle, a few minutes later, weighs in with *I don't care*.

At the bowling alley, we order burgers and fries to the lane, and the four of us are having a really good time. It's totally relaxed and fun, and the concern I had about Brett seems to have been unwarranted. Sunday night out with these three is the perfect way to spend the eve of the last chapter of our junior year of high school.

If only I were a better bowler. I pick up my ten-pound ball and approach the line. Danielle sits at the scorer's table, while Sloan and Brett occupy the bench behind her. When my ball heads directly into the gutter for the tenth time, I spin around and, if I'm not mistaken, I could swear I witness Sloan and Brett moving quickly and awkwardly away from each other. I shake my head like a cartoon cat trying to erase the image of the neighbor's bulldog.

"What's going on?" I ask suspiciously as I approach them.

"What are you talking about?" Brett asks. But it's obvious to me he knows exactly what I'm talking about.

"What are you talking about?" Danielle asks, no clue what I'm referring to.

I walk back to the bench, focusing on Sloan and Brett. "What's happening here?" I ask again.

"Nothing," Sloan says, but her poker face is the worst ever. I lock my eyes onto hers knowing she'll cave under the pressure.

"E.B. . . ." I prod.

"Nothing," she says again, and this time her face contorts into that distorted expression people make when they're trying not to smile. I don't say a word; I just stare at her, waiting for a confession. As predicted, she caves. She covers her face with her hands and starts laughing hysterically. Brett feigns exasperation at Sloan's lack of control, but his smile gives him away too.

I sit down on the bench next to them. "Start talking."

Brett and Sloan, practically completing each other's sentences, explain that they were the only two people home over spring break, and they started hanging out.

They use the time-tested clichés: *It just happened. We didn't plan it.*

"Oh my god, you had sex!" Danielle blurts out accusingly.

"No!" Sloan retorts.

"We're going to wait," Brett says with confidence.

"Yep," Sloan says. "We're going to wait."

"What exactly are you waiting for?" Danielle asks.

"Everyone we know who has done it has had some kind of regret or another," Brett says. "Either they rushed into it or they ended up breaking up and can't even look at the person anymore."

"Also," Sloan adds, "we don't need everyone at school talking about it. So we figured we'll wait till school ends. That way it's just about us: no gossip, no school politics, no bullshit."

"Well, that's only two months away," I say.

"No," Sloan says. "We mean till high school ends. Next year."

"Wow," Danielle and I say at the same time.

Now that the cat's out of the bag, the public display of affection begins in full force. Brett sidles up close to Sloan, putting one arm around her back and his other hand on her knee. He strokes her leg with his thumb, indicating a certain degree of possessiveness.

"Tell us more," Danielle practically begs. "When did you first kiss?"

"Last Friday," Sloan says and then turns to Brett. "It was Friday, wasn't it?"

"Yes, Friday." Now Brett is talking only to Sloan. "I picked you up at work and we stopped to get gas. You got out of the car to keep me company while the tank was filling up. You were leaning against the car and I just leaned against you and *boom!*"

Sloan smiles, riveted, like she's hearing this thrilling story for the first time. And, as if to recreate the magical memories, Brett tips his face close to hers and kisses her. I'm talking about a full French kiss that goes on longer than what is comfortable to observe. Danielle and I look at each other and share a surprised smile.

Brett seems different. Confident. He's lost a little of his edge in exchange for a peaceful happiness. Can it be that Sloan is making him shed his critical smugness? Was Sloan the answer all along?

Something definitely doesn't sit right here. Am I jealous? Wow, I think I might be a little bit jealous. Not that I want Brett. I don't. However, he's my best friend. I was the one who connected Sloan to Brett. I was the common denominator. And now, in seven short days, they have reached a degree of intimacy I could never share. And somehow their choice to wait to have sex makes their relationship seem even more real, more mature, more serious. I've been demoted.

I can say with one hundred percent honesty that I

want the best for Sloan and Brett. I definitely want them both to be happy. And if they can make each other happy, even better. It's just going to take some getting used to. I guess getting used to things is becoming a regular practice for me.

CHAPTER THIRTY-EIGHT

I**T'S PROM NIGHT.** Danielle and Sloan are at my house while I get ready. I feel like Cinderella with two fairy godmothers. Sloan is really good at make-up and I am not. She brought over her make-up bag—a huge black satchel with various compartments, zippers, and pockets. As she unpacks her products onto my bathroom counter, I can't discern the difference between the powders, creams, concealers, bronzers, blushes, and shadows. Sloan tells me I don't need to know and she'd like me to shut up and sit down.

Danielle is documenting the step-by-step process by taking photos on her phone. She also is the master DJ, picking the perfect music to set the tone for the evening.

"I want to look like me," I warn Sloan, afraid she's going to overdo it with the make-up.

"Please stop talking and do this," Sloan says, making a bizarre face where she pulls her chin and mouth down in an effort to expose her lower lashes.

"I don't want to look anything like that," I say, joking.

"Would you like me to stop? Because I can stop right now," Sloan threatens teasingly.

"You better be nice," Danielle cautions me, "or she'll turn you into a clown."

"Sorry," I say to Sloan. "Thank you for doing this. I love you so much."

"That's more like it," Sloan says.

Her final step is a shimmery pink lip gloss. Before deciding, she holds five different lip glosses and lipsticks up to my dress to select the perfect companion. Without letting me look in the mirror, Danielle and Sloan help me step into my dress and shoes. The only piece of jewelry I wear is the gold heart bracelet Luke gave me for Valentine's Day. Danielle releases my hair from the clip that has been holding the loose curls Sloan magically created with a curling iron.

At long last, my friends turn me to face the mirror, and I must say, I am thrilled with the end result. It's exactly how I wanted to look tonight. The significance of this evening is not just that it's Luke's prom. It seems that tonight is the final piece of our story. Next week is Senior Week, when the graduating class has parties, commencement rehearsals, and grad night. Meanwhile, I will be studying my butt off for final exams; junior-year report cards are hugely important for college applications. Luke and I will barely see each other next week, and then he will get on a plane for Boston. Tonight, with all its splendor, is in effect our farewell.

I have to pretend that Luke's leaving isn't absolute torture for me. I am determined to have fun tonight even though the truth of our impending goodbye rips my heart open every time I think of it, which is practically all the time. Luke and I barely discuss it. What's there to talk about? He's leaving and I love him. Those are the facts. The facts make me want to cry every day.

Most of Luke's friends have plans for overnight adventures to keep the prom going until the break of dawn. Some are having a giant sleepover, with both boys and girls, at a house in Coronado. Luke and I just want to be together as long as possible. My dad has a two-day trip to Chicago and St. Louis, and he won't be home until late Sunday night. That perfect little apartment with glorious views of the Pacific Ocean is empty.

I talked to Dad about my staying there after prom. He didn't even ask if that included Luke. He just said I'd have to discuss it with Mom. I treaded carefully.

"You know, a lot of people stay out all night," I said to my mother when the subject of the prom came up.

"I remember prom, Janey; it wasn't that long ago," she said. "Is there someplace you'd like to go?"

"There are after-parties and stuff," I said. "I'd actually like to stay at Dad's."

"That's fine," she said.

"Dad will be away." I felt the need to clarify.

"Oh," she paused. Like my dad, she didn't ask if Luke

was part of the plan. I think she's also taken on the *don't ask, don't tell* philosophy. "Let me think about it."

A couple of days later, she poked her head into my room.

"Hey," she said, trying to sound casual, "Dad and I talked about it, and it's fine if you want to spend the night there after the prom." The *you* could have meant just me, or me and Luke. I choose to assume it's fine for Luke to stay over. I also choose to keep my assumption to myself.

"Okay, thanks," I said, attempting to mimic her relaxed tone. Meanwhile, I was dying inside. Luke and I will have the chance to spend the whole night alone. I am definitely more excited about that part than I am for the prom itself.

Before Danielle and Sloan came over to help me get ready, I went over to Dad's and dropped off my stuff. I stopped at the market and bought some chocolate-chip cookies and vanilla-bean ice cream for tonight, as well as strawberries, croissants, and orange juice for tomorrow morning.

I am meeting Luke, Emily, and Zach at Luke's house for photos before the limousine picks us up. Luke's parents graciously invited my mom to share in the pre-prom festivities. My mom and I walk into the Hallstrom house as Luke comes down the stairs. I have always thought Luke was handsome. He's handsome in his track uniform and in blue jeans and a T-shirt. And I didn't think anything could be better than Luke naked. But Luke in a tuxedo is like nothing I have ever seen before. He is a dream.

His reaction to seeing me is what I hoped it would be. He stands at the foot of the stairs and just looks at me with an admiring grin. I think every girl in the world would want her boyfriend to look at her exactly that way.

"Peachy Keen, you look amazing," he says.

"So do you," I say back.

He escorts my mom and me to the backyard, where Luke's parents have set up a table with flutes of champagne and sparkling cider, and platters of appetizers. We all sip our drinks, take photos, exchange corsages and boutonnieres, and stand around with awkward smiles and already-sore feet until Luke finally announces that our limo has arrived.

The rest of the night is a blur as I hold Luke's hand though the pre-party, the prom, and an after-party at his friend Miles's house. We dance and kiss and take zillions of photos.

At about two in the morning, we find our way into my dad's apartment. I pull Luke back to my room and we kick off our shoes and collapse next to each other on the bed.

"That was so fun," he says.

"Best night ever," I agree.

"And the real fun hasn't even started yet," he says. He leans over me and puts his hand on my leg where the hem of my dress hits my thigh. "I love you in this dress," he says.

"You do?" I ask.

"I also love you out of this dress," he says.

I sit up and turn my back to Luke so he can unzip me. He takes his time lowering the zipper, revealing my braless back and pink underwear. He lifts my dress up and over my head and then lays me down on my stomach. Luke lies above me, resting on his elbows, and kisses me. He kisses the back of my neck, my shoulders, and my back. He works his way down, kissing every inch of my spine. He kisses across the waistband of my underwear, covering the entire span from hip to hip. Continuing to slowly lower himself, he covers my butt with tiny, soft kisses.

The feeling is astounding, like being brushed with velvety flower petals. With every kiss, I grow more relaxed and more turned on. I want him so bad, but waiting for it and knowing it's coming is exhilarating.

As he moves down my legs, kissing as he goes, he pulls my thong down with him. Slowly, slowly he goes, caressing the backs of my thighs and calves with his luscious lips. When he gets to my feet, he is at the bottom of the bed. He removes my underwear completely, then stands up and takes off his tuxedo, shirt, socks, and underwear. I stay in position, keeping my head on my pillow, but I recognize the sounds of the clothes being discarded and the condom wrapper opening.

Luke comes back to lie on top of me, his naked front to my back. I can feel him, hard and warm, between my legs. He rocks gently against me and I respond instinctively, meeting his movements. The rhythm, the tempo, the pace all perfectly in time. He lowers himself so his breathless voice is right in my ear.

"You're the sexiest girl out there." The words have an immediate effect on my body as I turn over and open my legs, making room for him to enter me. He starts slowly, moving ever so gently. But as the pleasure mounts, we move with more intensity. My hands clutch the pillows tightly and the sensations build inside my entire core.

Luke reaches under me with one hand on my butt and manages to flip us both over so that he's lying on his back with his head against the pillows and me on top of him. I straddle him and squeeze him tight with my legs while I hold on to his shoulders. I find the rhythm with my body to match Luke's breathing. I love having control of the movements, and I love knowing that the way I sway on top of him is causing the sounds of pleasure I hear escaping his lips. I want to feel our bodies pressed together, I want us to be entirely connected, so I lower my chest to his while I keep rocking my hips.

His face is above my shoulder, his warm sweet mouth at my ear. I hear his breathing get heavier, and my breaths quicken to match his. The feeling between my legs becomes almost too much to bear as his heart beats against my chest, pounding harder and harder. The heat, the rhythm, and the gasps between us escalate and I am about to shatter into an orgasm when I hear the faintest of whispers.

"Oh god."

A few minutes later, I walk naked into the kitchen and return with cookies, a carton of ice cream, and two spoons. Luke and I sit up in bed eating dessert and reliving prom night. We talk about Zach and Emily's absurd fight in the limo after he sat on her dress. We laugh about the terrible food served in the hotel ballroom. We realize that we both noticed Miles's parents trying lamely to spy on all the kids at the after-party.

Shortly after four in the morning, Luke and I drift off to sleep, holding each other tight, clutching each other with the knowledge that we can hold on tonight, but in the morning, we are going to have to let go. Let go for real. Maybe forever.

Despite my wishes, the sun does come up the next day and, in the harsh light of the morning, Luke and I look at each other with both satisfaction and sadness. We know we made the most of our time together. We were kind and respectful and honest. I learned so much from Luke —about myself, about sex, about growing up and falling in love. Luke taught me how to be adored and how to be vulnerable.

We sit at the little table in my dad's kitchen and sip orange juice. My croissant sits in front of me, but I can't stomach the idea of swallowing a single bite. I'm trying very hard to be upbeat, but I'm sad. I'm so very sad. I love him and I have to say goodbye. Maybe it's good to end on a high note. We won't have any memories of things going stale the way Danielle and Charlie's relationship did. We won't try to sustain a long-distance romance and suffer insecurity, jealousy, and paranoia. I will always love him like crazy.

Luke gets up and grabs a knife from the wooden block on my dad's kitchen counter. He brings the knife to the table and I assume he's going to cut his croissant, but instead he cuts the braided bracelet off his wrist. He scoots his chair next to mine, grabs my hand, and wraps the smooth brown leather around my wrist. He ties the ends into a tiny knot and grips one end with his teeth, pulling it tight.

"This thing has always been about you," he says.

"What do you mean?" I ask.

"I bought this on the beach the morning we were leaving Cabo. A few hours later, I saw you on the plane. For the two-hour flight, as I tried to get up the nerve to turn around and talk to you, I fiddled with this thing, tugging on the ends, ensuring its place on my arm. I stared at the leather braid, the whole time thinking about you sitting right there behind me."

"You wanted to talk to me on the plane?" I ask in disbelief. I can't imagine Luke ever having to psych himself up to speak to any girl, particularly me.

"Oh my god, yes," he says. "You were tan and your hair was pulled back and you looked so damn cute. And then you sang 'Wherever I Go' with no self-consciousness at all. And since then, everything has been about you. After we first kissed in my Jeep, as I drove home, I could swear this strip of leather smelled of you. Since I have had this, I have had you. I want you to wear it, because I want you to always have a piece of me."

"I love this," I say, running my finger along the worn leather.

"When you look at it, you'll remember me," he says.

"I don't need a bracelet to remember you," I assure him.

"Just wear it. Don't take it off."

"I won't. Ever. I promise."

CHAPTER THIRTY-NINE

G RADUATION CEREMONIES are about to begin. The graduating class is gathered on the football field, their caps and gowns shimmering in the spring sunlight. The orchestra's melody plays through the speakers as the graduates take their seats on the risers. Proud parents, grandparents, siblings, and friends plant themselves in white folding chairs.

Up above the field is a grassy hill. During football season, the hill catches the overflow of fans when the stands are jammed during Friday-afternoon games. The view is crappy, but you can hear the band and vaguely make out the numbers on the scoreboard.

Today, I sit on the hill with Danielle, Sloan, and Brett —my three best friends. We've seen one another through a lot this year. We've had bumps along the way, but here we are, watching commencement from a distance. Twelve months from now it will be us. And twelve months from tomorrow, we'll be going our separate ways. No one can predict all that will happen between now and then; however, I can say for certain that we will still be friends. I know we'll have fun, I know we'll have fights. There will definitely be sex, or *everything but*. And we can count on some surprises.

Down below where we sit, the valedictorian reads her speech into the microphone. We can't really make out the specific words, but the tone is clear. They've made it. The four hundred kids sitting down there in the sun have accomplished something significant. The speaker's voice conveys gratification, strength, and triumph. If the audience listens closely enough, they can probably also hear her self-satisfaction and superiority at being publically declared the smartest person on that football field. I wonder if she's had sex. Maybe she gets down and dirty with a guy from her AP Latin class. Maybe that cap, gown, and gold rope will be in a heap on the floor of that guy's car this afternoon.

Our principal begins reading the names of the class and each graduate rises to collect his or her diploma. The four of us lean back on our elbows, only vaguely aware of the individuals being mentioned. Then I hear it. Crystal clear. A shot ringing out through the silence.

"Luke Spencer Hallstrom."

I bolt upright. It's real. He's graduating. He's leaving. The gravity of it hits me hard, like a blow to the chest. Danielle, sensing my visceral reaction, wraps her arm around me and gives a little squeeze. Sloan, on my other side, leans her head on my shoulder.

The last of the names is called and, together, the graduating class, still standing, throw their mortarboards in the
air and let out an exuberant whoop. The joy is palpable.
The audience of loved ones claps and, no doubt, dabs at
a tear or two. I can see Luke finding his way to his mom
and dad. His brother and sister are there, too, and they all
stand together for a family photo. I watch Luke warmly
embracing his parents, his smile wide. He turns his head
this way. Is he looking for me?

"I guess I should go down there," I say, standing up and
dusting the grass from my skirt.

Brett nods.

"We'll wait here," Sloan says.

"Good luck," Danielle says.

And I begin the long walk down the hill to say hello.
And goodbye.

Acknowledgments

To Hannah Mann, thank you for holding my hand. You brought this book to life.

To Steven Malk, thank you for not laughing at me. You took a shot, and I am forever grateful.

To Elizabeth Bewley, thank you for jumping in. Your enthusiasm never wavered.

To Wendy Lefkon, thank you for being my friend. Your support knows no bounds.

Laura Hopper has worked in the film industry and is currently a book editor. *I Never* is her first novel. She lives in Los Angeles, California, with her family.